SUICIDE MISSION

Black Eagles commander Colonel Robert Falconi trotted forward with the Goons spread out on both sides of him. Directly to their front, the weapons squad of Second Commando moved as fast as possible under their load of machine guns. Threading their way through the NVA dead, they followed the rifle squads, ready to give them fire support.

The group had made twenty-five meters when the first mortar rounds hit.

Erupting in rapid blasts of orange flame and black smoke, the detonations sent out waves of concussions that buffeted the eardrums of Falconi and his men. Several of the ARVN rangers were bleeding from the ears as the world around them turned to a thundering, roaring hell. Shards of flying shrapnel sliced through men, cutting off bloody chunks in a horrible cloud of red spray and charred flesh.

Falconi knew there was no point in pulling back. The only thing that awaited them in the rear was more death and destruction. They had to charge ahead.

"Move on! Move on!" he ordered. "The man that stays here, dies here!"

BO-BINH COMMANDOS

THE BLACK EAGLES

JOHN LANSING

ZEBRA BOOKS
KENSINGTON PUBLISHING CORP.

ZEBRA BOOKS

are published by

Kensington Publishing Corp.
475 Park Avenue South
New York, NY 10016

First printing: May, 1990

Printed in the United States of America

This one is dedicated to

IDA WILSON

*From Falconi and the Guys
(with hugs and kisses from Archie Dobbs)*

Special Acknowledgement to Patrick E. Andrews

ORGANIZATION OF THE BLACK EAGLES
FOR OPERATION BO-BINH

COMMANDING OFFICER
Colonel Robert Falconi, *U.S. Army*

FIRST ASSAULT COMMANDO
Captain Ray Swift Elk, *U.S. Army*
Commander
Staff Sergeant Paulo Garcia, *U.S. Marine Corps*
Deputy Commander

SECOND ASSAULT COMMANDO
Sergeant Major Top Gordon, *U.S. Army*
Commander
Sergeant Steve Matsuno, *U.S. Army*
Deputy Commander

THIRD ASSAULT COMMANDO
Master Sergeant Malpractice McCorckel, *U.S. Army*
Commander
Sergeant Gunnar Olson, *U.S. Army*
Deputy Commander

MORTAR DETACHMENT
Chief Warrant Officer Calvin Culpepper, *U.S. Army*
Commander

GOON TEAM
Sergeant Loco Padilla, *U.S. Marine Corps*
Team Leader
Sergeant Archie Dobbs, *U.S. Army*
Goon
Petty Officer 3rd Class Blue Richards, *U.S. Navy*
Goon
Sergeant Ky Luyen, *South Vietnamese Army*
Goon

Prologue

The defensive line ran a jagged course through the dense jungle. The men who manned it—tough rangers of the Army of the Republic of South Vietnam (ARVN)—had dug in a scant two hours before. Now, with the evening shadows deepening fast, they worked to prepare themselves for what promised to be a long, monotonous night of interrupted sleep while following a dreary routine of shared sentry duty.

They were in a good mood.

American C-rations had been added to their supper that day. Mixed in with native rice, vegetables, and fruit from a mang-cau-dai tree, the meal had turned out to be delicious, particularly with the additional flavoring of indigenous condiments. The rangers, with full bellies, laughed and chattered as their entrenching tools slammed into the soft earth.

In the rear, the officers lounged around tables placed in large tents that had been pitched for them by a work detail of enlisted men. The mosquito nets were in place, and the food, well-cooked by a specially acquired kitchen crew, was served to them on expensive china dishes bought from a fund provided by their mess dues. Silverware that would have been the pride of any of the more select Saigon restaurants was also evident, as was good, chilled wine to go with the meal.

Most of these officers were from wealthy South Vietnamese families and had extra income outside of their meager army pay. They were a well-motivated group, serving in one of the roughest, most demanding units their country fielded in the war against the Communist North. Although as rugged as their men, they appreciated the extra touches of luxury even in the boondocks. That was why they retained the fine customs they had practiced in the French army, where most of them had served their military apprenticeships.

It all made sense to them. After all, just because an outfit was in the jungle was no reason why at least a few of the better things in life could not be brought along. That was the way the officers from France had lived, and it seemed a rather civilized way to run a war. It was neither overdemanding nor presumptuous on their parts that, following a day of mucking about in the dank mud of the rain forest and crossing streams where one got sopping wet, they enjoy a good dinner and wine. Not only was this a pleasant change in a grubby life, it was also a well-deserved reward for a job well done.

But out in the jungle, close by on the other side of the line where the rangers were dug in, were *un*civilized fighting men. They were as tough as the ARVN rangers and were quite content to live on nothing more exotic than boiled rice and water. They had no tents and only the barest of necessities for survival. These rugged combat veterans gave up comfort so that they could carry more weapons, ammunition, and grenades.

These were regulars of the NVA—the North Vietnamese Army.

The NVA troops had thrown homemade camouflage capes of palm fronds over their bodies and gone to ground. While the ARVN rangers prepared their lines, these Communists of the North listened to the chatter and digging sounds. Several hand-picked men had been detailed to go up into the treetops and draw rough but accurate sketches of the ARVN position. When they finished, these impromptu spies shimmied back down to the ground and hurried their art work to their commander, Major Tanh Hyun.

Hyun was a fast worker. He called his company commanders together and issued terse, easily understood orders in a calm voice. After everyone had synchronized their Soviet-made watches, these captains returned to their companies to brief their lieutenants and sergeants. Within a very brief time, the entire battalion knew the what, the when, the where, and the how of the upcoming operation.

The evening drifted on for a bit more. The reddening sun had sunk to the tops of the trees. It had been a tiring day, so a few of the rangers not scheduled for picket duty had already settled down to some much-needed sleep.

Then the steamy jungle exploded into a roaring hell of small arms fire and the enraged screams of attacking infantrymen.

The rangers stood stock still in shock and surprise. But only for an instant. Incoming salvos of 7.63 steel-jacketed slugs smacked into them, mowing the ARVN troops down in clumps of six to a full dozen. Attempts by the noncommissioned officers to rally a defense were useless in the bullet-filled hell of the jungle glen. The North Vietnamese infantry swept forward and over them in regulated waves while spraying death from their Kalashnikov AK47 assault rifles.

The first group of attackers swept on past the now devastated South Vietnamese MLR—Main Line of Resistance—and the second came in. Their job was to blast any survivors who still offered resistance. Firing sporadically at targets of opportunity, they also passed through the site of the initial clash, tailing after the primary assault force.

Finally the third wave came in. This bunch was less numerous and was made up of soldiers who were recovering from wounds or injuries but who were nonetheless still able to move about. The task assigned to them was a cruel one. Not wanting prisoners, the NVA commander's instructions were to dispatch any enemy wounded with quick shots to the head. These killers laughingly referred to themselves as the *quan-y*—the medical corps.

The front line of the NVA reached the officers' area. The South Vietnamese rangers had responded without hesitation to the sounds of battle. They rushed from their evening meal toward their personal tents for weapons. But the attack had moved in with such lethal swiftness that they were caught in the open. The Red infantry mowed them down with sweeping, hosing fire from their assault rifles. The ARVN officers were buffeted roughly in the metal hail, toppling to the ground in jerking piles of ripped flesh.

Six minutes after the assault had begun it was over.

Major Hyun, the NVA battalion commander, and his deputy, Captain Cuong Ngoi, walked forward through the piles of South Vietnamese dead. They noted the scattered corpses, some in clumps, that were strung out from the MLR clear back to the officers' tents.

Major Hyun lit a cigarette as he watched his men strip the ARVN dead of weapons, ammunition, and other useful items. "A quick victory, comrade."

Ngoi smiled. "Yes, Comrade Major. The complacency of the Southern soldiers cost them their lives." He glanced forward. "Ah! Here comes our intelligence officer. He has been searching the headquarters tent."

"Did you find anything of value?" Hyun asked as the man approached them.

"Yes, Comrade Major!" the lieutenant replied. "I have orders of battle, transportation schedules, and maps showing the exact locations of many enemy units."

Hyun gave the papers a quick perusal. He was so pleased that he chuckled. "These," he said to the other two officers, "will cost the lives of countless South Vietnamese and even American troops."

"Excellent, Comrade Major!" Ngoi said.

"Hurry the men up," Major Hyun said cheerfully. "We must press on to our next victory!"

Chapter 1

The name of the beach community was Hai-Cat, and by any civilized person's estimation it was heaven on earth. That is what one would expect of such a location in tropical environs.

Hai-Cat, however, was not an ordinary village by any standards. In actuality, it served as the home billet and headquarters of various Central Intelligence Agency bureaus and projects operating in Southeast Asia. Among those clandestine organizations was Colonel Robert Falconi's command, which in the late 1960s consisted of himself and eleven other individuals who showed a pronounced inclination toward violence. Various code names had been assigned Falconi's group from time to time. There had also been a few unofficial titles as well. For example, Brigadier General James Taggart of the United States Army had been known to refer to them as "pirates" when he was in a reasonably good mood. During outbursts of temper, the general usually spoke of them as "Falconi and those goddamned hoodlum bastards of his." But more often the detachment was respectfully called the Black Eagles, its permanent name, by those who came into contact with them.

And that was on *both* sides of the North-South conflict.

The Black Eagles had spent several tours billeted in a

remote Special Forces base camp called Nui-Dep. That particular little garrison was mortared with maddening regularity by the region's Viet Cong guerrilla force. It was located right in the middle of the war and seemed a handy place to deposit Falconi and the gritty guys who made up the detachment. It kept them out of the way and at a great distance from the broads and booze of the other units.

But, as luck would have it, the fortunes of war finally made it necessary to keep Falconi and his "goddamned hoodlum bastards" close at hand, where it would be easier to dispatch them to perform not only difficult missions but those also classified as impossible—or suicidal. Hai-Cat was a very nice location, and for this reason it seemed an unlikely place to post Falconi and his band of jungle fighters. The locale had been a rest and recreation center for the French army during a long period of time that stretched back over half a century. A few quaint villages made up of simple fisherfolk and peasant farmers were located nearby. They added to the placid atmosphere of the countryside that seemed so different from the shooting war raging around it.

Hai-Cat boasted a central administrative building where air conditioners hummed and quiet people concocted vicious tasks for other folks to perform. These jobs generally had something to do with killing (referred to officially as "neutralizing"), capturing (referred to officially as "acquiring"), or spying on (referred to officially as "monitoring") other individuals and groups who might or might not have a friendly disposition toward the United States forces and their allies participating in the Vietnam War.

Away from this den of devious planning and sneaky scheming, pleasant little bungalows were scattered around the grounds. Walkways led to these quarters, where people assigned to Hai-Cat lived. It was actually quite pleasant. Gentle, cooling breezes wafted through palm trees that stretched in groves down to a white, sandy beach washed by large, rolling swells from the deep blue South China Sea.

A breakwater of boulders had been built out from the seashore. It ran fifty meters past the surfline, forming a man-made lagoon. In those quieter waters, military and civilian transient boats used for intelligence missions were moored to a dock. There was also an old but reliable PBY Catalina amphibious plane tied to its proper place at the pier.

Near that location there was a recreational area that gave access to the water. It was there, on a very warm afternoon, that twelve hung-over men, accompanied by three rather attractive ladies, lay stretched out napping on beach towels while the effects of a heroic drinking bout slowly diminished, headaches drifting away through napping and quiet talk.

These individuals were Robert Falconi and his men, along with his lady-love Andréa Thuy. She was a lovely Eurasian woman who was part of their administrative team. Another of the women, Jean McCorckel, was a Vietnamese nurse married to the detachment medic. He was an overworked noncommissioned officer affectionately known as Malpractice McCorckel to the rest of the Black Eagles. The last woman, an African whose name was Uzuri Mwanamke, worked for the United Nations in dealing with war orphans. She was deeply involved with the unit's combat engineer.

The reason for their hangovers had been a celebration to recognize a couple of unexpected promotions. True, they had already feted the advancement of Sergeant First Class McCorckel to master sergeant and Sergeant First Class Calvin Culpepper's unexpected rise to chief warrant officer. But a few weeks later, promotion orders arrived that not only posted Lieutenant Colonel Robert Falconi to bird colonel but also elevated First Lieutenant Ray Swift Elk to the rank of captain. The latter was quite an accomplishment for a man who had only come off the Sioux Indian reservation in South Dakota at the age of seventeen, when he enlisted in the army.

These elevations in rank had to be celebrated, and it had been one hell of a party.

Blue Richards, a navy Seal from Alabama, spent his spare time producing white lightning whiskey on a regular basis from a portable still. This was a skill religiously practiced by the male members of his family. He moved his "likker-makin'" apparatus from time to time even though it wasn't really necessary. But after generations of being chased by tax revenuers from the Federal government, it was an ingrained habit the Alabamian had inherited from his ancestors.

Blue's whiskey was potent enough to keep the party going for a full three days and two nights before it finally wound down to just Colonel Falconi and Sergeant Archie Dobbs going drink-for-drink to see who would be the last Black Eagle standing.

It was to Archie's credit that right before he finally passed out, he managed to get to his feet and render a proper salute before falling flat on his face.

Now, with the buzzing in their heads subsiding, the Black Eagles lazed through the long afternoon. Archie Dobbs thoughtfully licked his lips and made a face. "I'd like to get my hands on that little dog."

Gunnar Olson, a Norwegian from Minnesota, looked up in curiosity. "What little dog, Archie?"

"The one that shit in my mouth last night," Archie replied still grimacing.

But the man who really suffered was the smallest one in the detachment. He was Sergeant Ky Luyen of the South Vietnamese army. A former Viet Cong who had defected, he'd done his damndest to go drink-for-drink with the larger Americans. The result had been an insanely drunk individual who had now sudsided to a limp, miserable fellow who was positive that being dead was a perfectly acceptable alternative to the agony he was enduring.

A couple of yards away from Ky, Top Gordon, the

detachment's top noncommissioned officer, scratched his hairy belly. He had a cooler full of beer at his elbow. "Are you sure nobody wants a brew?"

Ky almost puked thinking about it.

Steve Matsuno groaned. "I don't care if I never drink again."

Paulo Garcia chuckled. "You'll be talking different tonight."

"Pass me one o' them beers," Loco Padilla said. A marine like Paulo, he felt the honor of the Corps was at stake. "On second thought, you better gimme two or three."

"Ease off, Gyrene," Top growled. "I didn't take you to raise. You'll get one and like it."

Loco caught the one beer tossed to him and opened it. He took a drink and sighed. "So good!" He looked around. "Hey! Where the hell is Fagin?" He referred to Chuck Fagin, who was the Black Eagles' CIA case officer. He had been present when the festivities started but was nowhere to be seen at that moment.

Andrea Thuy laughed. "Are you just now missing him? He wasn't at the party long, y'know. Don't you remember him being called away?"

"I don't even remember being there myself," Loco said.

Archie Dobbs grinned. "Andrea, I don't remember who was and who wasn't there. If you told me that I was dancing with a lady wrestler, I'd have to believe you."

"You weren't dancing with one," Captain Ray Swift Elk said. "But I saw you go into the back room with one."

"Is that where I got them bruises?" Archie asked.

Loco Padilla took another drink of beer. "Hey!"

"What the hell's the matter?" Colonel Robert Falconi sat up. "It's harder than 'hell to get some sleep around here."

"Sorry, sir," Loco said. "But I just realized something. If Chuck Fagin was called from the party, who wanted to see him? When he ain't around, he's generally stirring up some shit for us."

Falconi became thoughtful. "Yeah." He nudged Andrea, who was Fagin's administrative assistant. "Just where is that boss of yours?"

"General Taggart called him to a conference and said it was damned important," Andrea said.

A unanimous shout of "Taggart?" erupted from the crowd.

Archie Dobbs groaned. "Well, boys, we'd better check them M16s and throw some C-rations in our rucksacks. We'll be heading back into the war as sure as shit stinks."

Somehow the hangovers now seemed even worse.

Chuck Fagin sat at the large conference table, his battered old canvas briefcase tucked under his chair. He doodled and wrote notes on the tablet in front of him. Several other officers, both American and South Vietnamese, occupied the rest of the chairs.

A speaker stood at the head of the room in front of an operational map. He was a trim, tough-looking colonel from the Army of the Republic of Vietnam named Long Kuyen. He had been educated in America and attended several U.S. Army staff courses. His English was perfect. The ARVN officer sported jump wings and the ranger badge of his country. Although he spoke in a calm voice, the news he gave was about as bad as news can get.

"Two companies of ARVN rangers were wiped out to the last man thirty-six hours ago," he announced. "I am sorry to inform you that this is not the first time this has happened in their particular operational area."

"Which one is that?" Chuck Fagin asked.

"It is called Bo-Binh," Kuyen answered. "The rangers out there have taken a terrible drubbing in spite of good equipment, good men, and good morale." He shook his head and shrugged. "Frankly, gentlemen, we cannot understand it."

"Neither can we," tersely interrupted Brigadier

General James Taggart. "And that's what this meeting today is all about. The situation has to be brought back under control—and goddamned fast, too! That is a part of Vietnam that guarantees security for the western campaigns."

"I have assigned my best officers to that area," Kuyen said. "All are tough, brave, and determined. But I must admit that many times they are careless about such things as noise and intelligence security."

Chuck Fagin lit a cigar. As he dropped the match in the ashtray in front of him he asked, "How many men have you lost out there?"

"More than two hundred," Kuyen answered. "And that includes several units completely wiped out. They were annihilated. Massacred!"

"Who the hell are they going up against?" General Taggart demanded to know.

"The intelligence is quite sketchy," Kuyen said with a sigh. "But there is no doubt they are not Viet Cong guerrillas. They are elite infantry troops of the North Vietnamese Army."

"Damn!" Taggart complained. "They move around the goddamned jungle like they own the stinking place!"

"As of right now, General," Fagin said lazily, "they most certainly do. And as landlords they're charging exorbitant rent."

"The enemy morale is high," Colonel Kuyen added. "They are either damned close to being undefeatable or soon will be. The situation is grave and dangerous to the greatest extreme. I speak both tactically and strategically. That area of the war is almost lost. As General Taggart said, that opens up the entire western flank to almost unceasing attack."

"Pardon me for saying so, Colonel Kuyen, but we may have a problem with leadership in your unit," Taggart suggested.

"I would be the first to admit it," Kuyen said.

"Little things can mean a hell of a lot," the general

17

went on. "What we need there are some advisers to set some standards and give a few lessons to set things right." He was thoughtful for a few moments while the other officers waited for him to continue. Finally he said, "Regular infantry officers couldn't pull it off. Not even ranger-qualified ones. This is an unconventional puzzle calling for an unconventional solution." He looked over at Major Rory Riley. "What about your outfit, Riley?"

Riley, the commander of the Green Beret detachment at Nui-Dep, where the Black Eagles used to live, only shrugged. "Sorry, sir. My men are already deeply committed to Operation Thunderbird. I've barely got enough in camp to mount a decent defense in case of attack."

"Yeah," Taggart said.

Riley shook his head. "Even if I had the people to spare, I wouldn't be very enthusiastic about it. The mission sounds like a no-win situation. Whoever goes in probably won't be coming out."

Taggart nodded. "That's right." He swung his eyes to Chuck Fagin and grinned. "Tell me, Fagin old boy, just what the hell is Falconi and those goddamned hoodlum bastards of his up to these days?"

"You mean the Black Eagles?" Fagin asked.

"I don't mean the Lennon Sisters, buster!" the general said with a wicked grin.

Chapter 2

The column of men, made up of two files, double-timed in perfect step to Sergeant Major Top Gordon's shouted cadence:

"Hut-foh! Hut-foh! Hut-foh!"

The Black Eagles, winding up their morning physical training with a five-mile run, were sweat-soaked in the tropical heat. Dressed in T-shirts, shorts, and jump boots, they moved with military precision despite their fatigue. To increase the challenge of the ordeal, the sergeant major saw to it that they did their running on the beach, where the sand made movement much more difficult.

While the sergeant major trotted alongside them, the column was led by Colonel Robert Falconi and Captain Ray Swift Elk. Falconi's near fanatical devotion to physical fitness was shared by his men. Each duty day morning began with a strenuous hour of hard physical exercise topped off by the breath-searing run. Three times a week they went out in the hottest part of the day with a full combat load to run again in the afternoon, holding M16s alternately at high port and over their heads.

Regular units did not permit that sort of strenuous activity in such a combination of high temperature and humidity. But Falconi reasoned that if they had to fight in such a steamy environment, the Black Eagles had

19

damned well be able to perform their exercises in the same kind of weather.

"Column left, *march!*" Top commanded.

The detachment turned in that direction and came out of the beach sand stepping onto the macadam of the roadway. Now the loud, scratchy staccato of their boots striking the ground in unison echoed among the palm trees.

As they neared their headquarters, Top issued another command. "Quick time, *march!*"

They immediately slowed into a regular marching rate, stepping out with backs straight and heads up.

"Forty inches all around, goddamnit!" Top bellowed. "You look like a bunch o' basic training rookies!"

Everyone dressed right and covered down to bring their formation into the sergeant major's concept of what a properly formed military group is supposed to look like.

"Detachment, *halt!* Right, *face!* At ease!" Top ordered. "Malpractice is going to hold a sick call right after you take your showers. How many sick-lame-and-lazy do we have?"

Steve Matsuno, who had badly bruised his arm in a karate drill with Colonel Falconi, raised his hand. So did Blue Richards. He had burned his hand slightly while cooking up his latest batch of white lightning.

"Oh, shit!" Archie said.

Top glared at the detachment scout. "Who gave you permission to talk?"

Archie ignored the question as he pointed up toward their headquarters building. "Look, guys. It's Chuck Fagin."

Even Top quickly looked over at the doorway. Fagin, their CIA case officer, waved back with a sly grin on his Irish face. He was obviously waiting for them. Fagin held his battered old canvas briefcase in his hand. Nodding his head, he pointed to it. That inelegant container always held the operations plans and orders of Black Eagle missions. The sight of it to the detachment was like showing a shotgun to a well-trained hunting dog. The canine knew things were about to happen.

"Goddamn!" Paulo Garcia said. "I'll bet he's got paperwork on a real hairy mission in there."

"You bet," Archie said. "You can tell by that shit-eating grin on his face."

"Yep," Blue said. "No doubt it means we'll be heading out to the big bad war again."

"Yeah," Calvin Culpepper agreed. "And it'll be good to get the kinks out, believe me."

Top snapped his head back around. "Quiet in the ranks!" Even though he was a noncommissioned officer, outranked by Colonel Falconi, Captain Swift Elk, and Warrant Officer Culpepper, he was in charge of the formation. When Sergeant Major Top Gordon said to shut up he meant for *everybody* to shut up. "Detachment, tinch-*hut!* Dismissed!"

Before breaking formation and heading inside, the Black Eagles took deep breaths and shouted their unit motto, "Calcitra Clunis!" The Latin words translated literally as "Kick Ass!"

Falconi, Swift Elk, and Calvin, the unit's officers, walked over to where Fagin waited for them.

"Hi, Chuck," Falconi greeted him.

"What's shaking?" Calvin Culpepper asked.

"A whole lot, Calvin," Fagin said. He nodded to Swift Elk. "How's it going, Ray?"

"Pretty good," Ray Swift Elk answered. "What have you got for us?"

"It's something you've never been involved in before," Fagin said. He made a face as he smelled the three sweating men. "But I believe there's time for you guys to take showers before we get together."

"Sure," Falconi said. "And after we're all clean and dainty, will it be your place or mine, lover?"

"My place," Fagin said. "Andrea is putting together some kits for everybody now."

"We'll see you in a bit," Falconi said.

The colonel, the captain, and the chief warrant officer went on into the billets. After stripping off in their room and grabbing shower kits, they went down to the latrine, where the rest of the detachment was already finishing up their own bathing.

Sergeant Major Top Gordon, his hairy body a stark contrast to the sparseness of hair on his head, toweled himself dry. "What's Fagin got on line for us, sir?"

"He didn't give us any details," Falconi said stepping under the fast-flowing water.

Calvin Culpepper let the warm water wash away the sweat. "He was the same ol' mysterious Fagin."

Ray Swift Elk got under his own faucet. "But he said it's a sort of operation that we've never pulled off before."

"Hey! That must mean we'll be well supplied!" Gunnar Olson yelled.

"And that we'll have cold beer!" Archie Dobbs hollered.

"With a good chance of not getting our asses blowed away!" Blue Richards added.

"And cold beer and women, too!" Archie Dobbs hollered.

Paulo Garcia laughed. "And things will go smooth and easy for a change."

"And cold beer and women and hot chow!" Archie Dobbs hollered.

"You guys knock off the bullshit," Falconi said. "And stand by. Calvin, Ray and I are going to see our friend Fagin as quick as we get done here."

"Yeah," Ray Swift Elk said. "We'll get the bad news to you just as soon as we can."

"But we'll be gentle about it," Calvin promised as he soaped up.

A full two hours passed as the Black Eagles waited impatiently in their billets. Some, like Archie and Blue, lay on their bunks and took advantage of the lull in procedures to catnap. Ky Luyen and Loco Padilla, on the other hand, paced a bit and carried on a lively conversation.

Finally the door opened and Calvin Culpepper stepped inside. "The old man wants to see ever' swinging dick. Bring notebooks and pens 'cause there's gonna be a lot of notes to take. Move it!"

"Yes, sir!" they shouted.

Within short moments they crowded after Calvin who led them down the hall to the briefing room. When they entered they saw that Andrea Thuy and Chuck Fagin were standing there with Falconi and Ray Swift Elk.

"Sit down, quickly," Falconi said. He waited for his men to settle in. Andrea immediately walked among them passing out manila folders containing a typed document.

Falconi waited for his men to give him their undivided attention. "As we all knew, Chuck has come back with a mission for us to perform. And it is a most different sort of mission, gentlemen."

"What's going down, sir?" Steve Matsuno asked. The Japanese-American was Falconi's favorite karate sparring partner. Although he called Oakland, California his hometown, he'd been born in one of the internment camps in Arizona during World War II.

"We're used to going in on our own and fighting the good fight as a lone detachment," Falconi explained. "But this time we're going to take command of an ARVN ranger group and lead units of those guys as their commanders."

"What brought this about?" Malpractice McCorckel asked.

Fagin interjected. "There's a slight problem with the ARVN officers. They need a bit of guidance, and General Taggart figured you were the guys that could do it."

"Shit!" Archie said. "You mean he figures we're the guys he don't mind getting killed doing it."

"That could be right, too," Fagin said.

"But aren't we going to do like we always do?" Archie Dobbs asked. "Study the OPLAN and rewrite it for a brief-back?"

"Negative," Falconi said. "We're going to be about as conventional as we can be. I am going to brief you here and now, then we're going in and pull this thing off."

Andrea Thuy went to the rear of the room and sat down. She had been on plenty of combat operations herself and she knew how anxious the men would be to find out the scoop on the latest mission.

"Where are we going?" Blue Richards asked.

"We'll be headed for a nasty place known officially as Operation Area Bo-Binh."

"What the hell is the situation out there, sir?" Top Gordon wanted to know.

"The big sad fact is that there are no friendly troops in OA Bo-Binh," Falconi said. "An elite infantry battalion of the North Vietnamese Army owns the territory, which stretches to the northwest between Tay Ninh and An Loc."

Malpractice McCorckel was offended. "Now how the hell did all that happen?"

"They wiped out or drove away all the ARVN units that faced them in the area," Falconi said. "And I don't mean outfits made up of ill-trained conscripts. I am talking about hardcore, elite, motivated, squared away, bad-ass ARVN rangers!"

"Shit!" Archie Dobbs said.

"Yeah," Falconi said. "Shit! And our job is going to be to turn that situation around."

"Just what the hell are we going to do, sir?" Gunnar Olson asked.

"Okay," Falconi said. "Here's the word. We are going to link up with a South Vietnamese ranger unit. I am going to be in command overall and you guys will be the subunit leaders. I am going to divide the rangers into commandos. When that is done, we'll move into the operational area and set up for a conventional war situation to defeat the NVA battalion that is now firmly set up there."

"What's your idea of a commando?" Loco Padilla inquired. *Commando* was a sort of ambiguous military term that could mean almost anything.

"They'll each be made up of three rifle sections with a machine gun section for fire support," Falconi answered.

"But exactly how are you going to organize us, sir?" Paulo Garcia asked.

"Listen up," Falconi said. "The First Assault Commando will be commanded by Ray Swift Elk. His deputy commander will be Paulo. The Second Commando will be led by Top with Steve Matsuno as his second-in-command. The Third will have Malpractice as the honcho with Gunnar working under him. Finally, Calvin Culpepper will be the commanding officer of the mortar detachment."

"What kind of tubes are me and my boys gonna be shooting out of, Colonel?" Calvin asked.

"81-millimeter," Falconi answered. "So you can see that we'll be able to call in pretty good fire support when we need it."

"And you'll need it!" Calvin said with a grin.

"Just a minute, sir!" Loco Padilla protested. "You left some of us out!"

"Hold your goddamned horses!" Falconi said. "I'm not going to go *completely* conventional. I want to keep some of our old ways in the picture too. So we'll have a Goon Team with Loco as the leader. He'll have Archie Dobbs, Blue Richards, and Ky Luyen as his goons."

Ky was glad to be in a special unit. "Just what we do, Colonel?" he asked in his broken English.

"Whatever nasty little things need doing," Falconi answered. "Special combat or recon patrols, raids, grabbing prisoners, and generally acting in a manner completely contrary to the commonly held standards of human decency."

"Sir, I resemble that remark!" Archie said.

"So," Falconi continued. "You'll take a normal combat load with you when we leave here in the morning. We depart 0600 hours aboard the PBY. We should arrive at the rendezvous point at an air field near Tay Ninh at approximately 0715 hours."

"Wait a minute, sir!" Steve Matsuno called out. "That aircraft is in the water at the dock. How're we gonna land her at an airfield?"

"It's an amphibious plane," Falconi said. "That means it can be operated on land or water, Steve."

"Thank you, sir," Steve said. "I wish we'd get more modern aircraft so a guy would know what he was dealing with."

"Not to worry," Falconi said. "At any rate, when we arrive we'll meet the rangers and begin the coordination and reorganization into our three commandos and mortar section."

"Don't forget the Goons!" Archie Dobbs called out.

"Yes," Falconi said. "And the Goons, too."

"What about commo, sir?" Malpractice McCorckel asked.

"Each of you commanders will have a ranger radioman sticking close by you at all times," Falconi said. "He'll be toting an AN/PRC-77 with a handset for voice broadcast."

"At least we won't have to go through coding and encoding with CW," Blue Richards said.

"Sir?" Loco Padilla asked holding up his hand. "Are us goons going to have a radioman too?"

"Ky will take care of you," Falconi said. "But you are also to have a ranger assigned to you as a regular goon."

Fagin interrupted. "They're going to pick a good one for you, Loco. The ARVN commander told me that he would send one of his best fighting men."

"That's good," Loco said. "What about call signs on the radio?"

"I will be Checkmate," Falconi said. "Commando One is Checkmate One, Commando Two is Checkmate Two, and guess what Commando Three will be?"

"Checkmate Three!" Ky Luyen called out. He failed to grasp the fact it was a rhetorical question. Everyone laughed.

"Right, Ky," Falconi said. "The Mortar Section will be Checkmate Four and the Goons are Checkmate Five. Any more questions?" When there were none, he said, "Sergeant Major, take over the detachment."

"Yes, sir!" Top said getting to his feet. "What are you guys hanging around here for? You got patrol harnesses and weapons to tend to. There's a great big fucking war out there, and it's just waiting for us."

Chapter 3

The Asian man was known to his American friends as Choy. Actually, his family name was Chieu, but "Choy" was as close as they could come to that. From the rather battered condition of Choy's face, he appeared to be a professional pugilist. It was quite easy to see that his flat, slightly misshapen nose had been broken more than just a few times, and the pronounced scar tissue around his eyebrows gave evidence of closed-over gashes. His build, heavy in the shoulders and a bit thin in the shanks, was also a natural one for a fighter. In fact, at one time in his life Choy had been a champion kick-boxer. Some people might consider him somewhat rough looking and perhaps even menacing or threatening, but when he smiled or spoke, his good humor and high intellect became obvious.

And, indeed, Choy was an educated and cultured man. Actually, his fighting career had been short-lived. Because he came from an upper-class, educated Chinese family, his father forced him to withdraw from the sport and continue getting an excellent education, as was expected of him. The result was that, after a comfortable but boring stint flying with Taiwan Airlines, he now held a position with the CIA's Air America as a navigator. To add to his excitement, this scion of a wealthy Asian family flew with two wild Irishmen.

The pilot's name was Tim Donegan. He was a man who swilled Guinness Stout with near-religious fanaticism. He did more than just enjoy the thick, rich, malty flavor of the drink, he reveled in it. Although a heavy imbiber, Donegan was reputed to be able to put anything with wings and a motor into the air. He had retired from the navy as a chief petty officer with the distinction of being one of the last enlisted pilots on active flight status.

Their mechanic, a perennial tough guy named Mike McKeever, was also a retired sailor. A hell of a big man, McKeever stood six-feet-four and topped out at two hundred and forty pounds. He carried a paunch built up from years of trying to keep up with Donegan's consumption of Guinness. He was a damned good mechanic, but he'd never been able to hold much rank in the navy. He had been rated an aviation machinist mate second class for a short period of time and took the test for first class on no less than seven occasions. But between a short attention span and a shorter temper, his conduct rating was not the highest. Although not actually stupid, he sometimes had a difficult time reading, writing, and expressing himself verbally. Communication was not one of McKeever's strong points. That was why he loved to tinker with engines. Once he was inside one, it all seemed to sing out to him, telling the mechanic all its innermost secrets and problems. Motors liked Mike McKeever and he liked them.

The aircraft the trio drove was a Catalina PBY-5A Amphibian. Complete with gun stations—waist, nose, and a rather strange one called a "tunnel" that fired rearward and downward from a position under the tail—she carried bomb racks and was powered by a pair of Pratt and Whitney R-1830-92 engines that generated twelve hundred horsepower. A versatile craft that served the sneaky purposes of the CIA or any other intelligence group that needed her, she was kept in tip-top running shape through McKeever's efforts.

On that particular humid morning, the PBY's crew—

Donegan, Choy, and McKeever—stood at the Hai-Cat's dock waiting for the arrival of their passengers. Choy had already charted out the course, so he would simply ride along and check things out to keep Donegan on the right flightpath. McKeever, besides having to keep the engines humming, was also responsible for the interior of the troop compartment. He made sure it was ready to seat and contain the Black Eagle Detachment and all their gear comfortably.

They hadn't waited more than fifteen minutes before a dozen combat-equipped troopers appeared in single file from the treeline by the billeting area. Colonel Falconi and his men continued across a narrow strip of white sand and stepped up on the dock. The colonel led his detachment down to the aircraft.

"Hi, Falconi," Donegan said. "At it again, huh?"

"Yeah," Falconi said walking up. He dumped his ruck-sack, weapon, and other gear to the pier. "This trip is going to be sort of boring for you fellows, isn't it?"

Choy laughed. Although he had many years of schooling and study, he had never quite mastered the English language. "You betcha, Falconi! Last time we see you, Russian tanks chase your asses across Cammon Plateau in Laos."

McKeever didn't smile. "We thunked you was goners."

"Well, you *thunked* wrong, didn't you?" Falconi said. He turned to Top. "Sergeant Major, get 'em aboard."

"You'll be goners one o' these days," McKeever said bluntly. "You Black Eagles are crazier 'n hell. Where you going this time?"

"It's classified," Falconi said. "All you have to know is to land us at Tay Ninh."

"I got a clearance," McKeever insisted.

"Yeah, but you don't have the Need-To-Know," Falconi said.

Tim Donegan was disappointed. "Is all we're gonna do is drop you off at the airfield?"

"That's it, Tim," Falcon said.

"Maybe we should stick around," Donegan suggested. "Sometimes you guys need a little air support."

"I'll keep that in mind, but there's been no arrangements to keep you guys handy," Falconi said.

"We're at loose ends right now, so we ain't got a hell of a lot to do. We'll check in with Fagin now and then," Donegan said.

"I'd appreciate that," Falconi said. He knew that if the Black Eagles needed air support it would be low-level combat support. He also knew that Tim Donegan was one crazy-assed pilot, a guy who would brush the tree tops to get the job done.

The colonel waited until the last man climbed through the clamshell opening to the fuselage's interior. He leaned down and picked up his gear.

"I'm not bullshitting, Falconi. Don't forget to give us a call if the situation starts to bring hot scalding piss all over you out there, huh?" Tim said.

"Yeah," McKeever said pointing to the devices under the wings. "Them's bomb racks, y'know."

"I know," Falconi said winking. "And I'll keep that offer in mind. At any rate, we're glad you're giving us this ride."

"You call, we haul," Tim said.

"You sass, we kick ass," McKeever added.

"You ask us and we give you some help," Choy said, trying to keep the thought going but not quite understanding how to manipulate the English language.

Falconi stepped inside and saw that his men were already buckled in. He arranged himself properly as McKeever joined the passengers.

"Okay, guys!" McKeever called out. "Next stop, Tay Ninh."

As soon as the mechanic settled down for the ride, the engines sputtered a couple of times, then kicked to life. The big aircraft rocked a bit as it swung in the placid waters of the man-made lagoon. After running up the motors for a quick test, Donegan started the big bird on its way toward the breakwater for takeoff.

Archie Dobbs smiled weakly at Blue Richards. "Back to the wars."

"I hope we ain't gone long," Blue remarked. "I think I left the fire burnin' under my moonshine still."

The landing at the air field was routine, as was the unloading. Tim Donegan kept the port engine running as he feathered back starboard to keep the propeller blast down as the Black Eagles crawled through the side blister windows with their gear. At a wave-off signal from Falconi, the pilot kicked the motor back to life and taxied away for takeoff to return to Hai-Cat.

Colonel Long Kuyen of the ARVN rangers was on hand to meet them. After an exchange of salutes and quick introductions all around, he was ready to take the Black Eagles out to their new unit. He'd brought a jeep and deuce-and-a-half truck with him for transportation.

"The enlisted men will ride in the back of the truck," Kuyen announced. "The three officers will please accompany me in the jeep."

Within moments the two-vehicle convoy roared off the runway and out onto the road leading to the highway. The ARVN drivers lived up to their wild reputation by manhandling the vehicles at breakneck speed through market areas and a small village before turning onto a rural road and racing down the narrow track toward their garrison.

The ranger camp was symmetrically correct. They had no permanent buildings, only tents of various sizes. The canvas shelters presented a martial view. They were laid out in straight lines, dressed right and covered down with the precision of a parading battalion. The South Vietnamese flag flew proudly on a tall staff in front of the headquarters tent.

Falconi was not impressed.

"Excuse me, Colonel Kuyen," he said leaning toward

32

the ARVN officer. "I strongly suggest that your camp be broken into irregular patterns. Stark, straight lines attract the eye in a rural setting. It is not nature's way to be so regular and precise."

Kuyen smiled. "A good suggestion, Colonel Falconi. This is a practice we learned from the French."

Chief Warrant Officer Calvin Culpepper pointed. "Those whitewashed rocks also attract the eye, Colonel."

The small white boulders were used to line paths between headquarters and some of the larger tents. "That is done to create an atmosphere of military precision," Kuyen said. "Besides, we do not have to worry about aerial surveillance. Our enemies do not possess aircraft."

"Yes, sir," Calvin said carefully. "But their forward observers for their mortars climb trees—*tall* trees!"

"A good point," Kuyen said.

The two vehicles came to a dust-swirling, noisy stop in front of headquarters. Back on the truck, Top Gordon set the men into motion and had them hop off to form up and wait for orders.

The officers stepped out of the jeep. Colonel Kuyen pointed to some nearby tents. "The large one is the officers mess," he announced. "The medium sized ones are quarters for officers. Three have been set aside for you, Colonel Falconi, and Captain Swift Elk, and Mister Culpepper as well."

"What about the rest of my men?" Falconi asked.

"They will be taken care of immediately," Kuyen said. "Here comes my senior noncommissioned officer."

A tough-looking ranger, wearing the three gold chevrons of a chief sergeant, literally paraded up to them. He came to a foot-stomping halt and saluted. "Chief Sergeant Quan Hao reporting, sir!"

"Chief Sergeant, take the enlisted men down to the soldiers' billeting area."

Falconi interrupted. "Just where is that?"

"There, Colonel," Kuyen said pointing.

Falconi looked in the indicated direction and saw rows

of two-man pup tents. "My men are to sleep there?" he asked.

"Yes," Kuyen said.

"And myself and my officers there?" he asked pointing to the larger tents. Each had a table, chair, and a bunk with sheets. They were luxurious in comparison with the soldiers' living facilities.

"Of course, Colonel," Kuyen answered.

Falconi shook his head. "I beg your pardon, Colonel Kuyen. But officer and enlisted man separation is not part of my military philosophy. At least not in units such as mine, Special Forces, and—excuse me—rangers. Those customs may bode well in regular line outfits, but they are completely out of place in unconventional warfare."

Kuyen was surprised. "Really, Colonel?"

"I'm most serious," Falconi assured him. "Do your officers eat the same food as your men?"

"Of course not, Colonel," Kuyen replied. "We even enjoy good wine in our officers mess."

"By your leave, Colonel," Falconi said. "My two officers and I will eat with our men and also billet with them in the same area and the same type shelters."

"Of course, Colonel Falconi," Kuyen said. "I understand. I do not wish to impose on your unit's procedures in any way."

A bugle suddenly sounded in close proximity. It was mess call. An immediate surge of activity took place in the camp as the ranger battalion prepared for their midday meal.

"I will meet you at headquarters after chow," Falconi said. He turned toward the men by the truck. "Sergeant Major Gordon! Move the men out for chow. We'll eat our C-rations down by the creek there." He turned to Colonel Kuyen. "Until later, Colonel."

"Of course, Colonel," Kuyen said saluting.

The headquarters tent was crowded. In spite of having

full bellies on a warm afternoon, everyone there was wide awake and eager. Both Black Eagles and picked individuals from the ARVN ranger battalion were present. They were all well-trained troops, knowing that within a very short time they would be back in the war to perform an extremely hazardous mission. No attempt had been made to minimize the truth or facts about the great dangers they faced. Yet not one would have withdrawn from the operation if offered the chance.

Colonel Robert Falconi had the floor. "Gentlemen, as everyone now knows, we are going to break down into various commandos. Each of these units will be led by members of my detachment, with a South Vietnamese ranger attached for liaison and assistance in command. As I introduce my cadres, I would appreciate it if the ARVN ranger assigned to them would make his own introduction. The First Commando will be led by Captain Ray Swift Elk, with Staff Sergeant Paulo Garcia as his deputy."

A ranger captain stood up. "I am Captain Huy. It is my honor to be assigned as the liaison to that commando."

"Second Commando will be led by our senior non-commissioned officer, Sergeant Major Top Gordon. He will be assisted by Sergeant Steve Matsuno."

Chief Sergeant Quan Hao, whom they had met earlier, came forward and joined the two Black Eagles.

"Master Sergeant Malpractice McCorckel and Sergeant Gunnar Olson will head up the Third Commando," Falconi announced.

A young ranger lieutenant, grinning in happy anticipation, walked up to the front of the room. "I am Lieutenant Gyo. I shall act as Third Commando liaison officer. Thank you."

Falconi continued. "Our mortar section will be under the command of Chief Warrant Officer Calvin Culpepper."

"I am Adjutant Nguyen," a South Vietnamese warrant officer announced. He walked up to Calvin, offering his hand. "I, too, am an expert in mortars."

"Glad to have you with me," Calvin said sincerely.

"And last is our special unit," Falconi said. "The Goons. These men are going to handle particularly nasty and dangerous assignments." He introduced Loco Padilla, Archie Dobbs, Blue Richards, and Ky Luyen.

A short, husky ranger, sporting the insignia of a corporal, walked up. "I am Trang Ngo," he said. "I like to kill Viet Cong and North Vietnamese." He said it as if he were discussing a favorite sport.

"You'll fit in good with these badasses, Corporal Ngo," Falconi said. "Now I have some announcements. They are important because they cover exactly how we're going to be running this operation."

The Vietnamese officers were particularly interested in what the American colonel was going to say. They knew it would affect the arrangements between themselves and their men during Operation Bo-Binh.

"There will be no more pup tents," Falconi said, "or any other kind of tents. They will all be left behind here when we go to the operational area. When a command post is set up, it will be under a tree or in some other handy spot. If necessary we can string up a poncho overhead. There will be no more mess calls. Everyone will eat C-rations. So all the cooks will report to the line. And this strike force will go immediately into isolation. I want no more contact between the soldiers and their families or nearby villages."

"I will post guards and seal off our camps," Colonel Kuyen said.

"Thank you," Falconi said. "Tomorrow's activities will be the firming up of organization into commandos. And we'll have a few quick run-throughs on assault and defense techniques to give us a chance to get used to working together. Are there any questions?"

The men were all silent.

"Then let's get to work, gentlemen," Falconi said grimly. "In forty-eight hours we're going to be up to our ears in a real, bloody shooting war."

Chapter 4

The South Vietnamese rangers walked easily, almost gracefully, as they entered the jungle. With their normal combat load lightened by twenty-five percent through the American Colonel Falconi's direction, they felt more mobile. They were no longer encumbered by horseshoe-rolled shelter halves, blankets, or mess kits. The tough soldiers grinned at each other, particularly when they noticed their officers now carried their own gear as well. And there were no strength-draining tasks required to transport the big tents and kitchen for the rankers, either.

Morale and confidence soared with what they considered a novel approach to field soldiering.

The only unhappy rangers were those who had enjoyed the limited luxury of stints as officers' orderlies and cooks. They were now firmly established back in their rifle or machine gun squads, once again earning their monthly piasters as fighting men rather than servants.

And all the rangers—officer and enlisted—carried only patrol harness with ponchos, poncho liners, entrenching tools, grenades, ammo, a couple of changes of socks, and their weapons.

All their other gear had been left behind at the base camp, where a detail of guards made up of convalescing troops kept an eye on things. Rations, ammunition, and other items of supply would be forwarded as needed. While such an arrangement was not that unusual for the rangers, this system of resupply was a downright luxury as far as the Black Eagles were concerned. Most of their operations took place behind enemy lines, well out of the reach of most military service channels.

The Vietnamese radio operators each toted one of the twenty-plus-pound AN/PRC-77 radios. They stuck close to the Black Eagle commando leaders in case the need for a transmission became necessary.

The Goon Team had been sent into the area first. During an initial scout they made sure the area was clear of enemy troops or any nasty things the NVA might leave behind—booby traps, mines, or snipers. Loco Padilla and his handpicked men did their job well. As each commando approached, the team leader detailed one of the Goons to act as guide to lead the unit to its place in the line. Within the short space of twenty minutes the entire strike force was well situated and beginning the task of digging in.

Finally, one-by-one, the reports came back via radio to Falconi:

"Checkmate, this is Checkmate One," Ray Swift Elk said. "Calcitra Clunis." Falconi, wanting to minimize transmission time in case of enemy communications monitoring, decided to use the detachment motto as a quick way to indicate each commando was in position and setting up.

"Roger," Falconi replied through his radio transmitter. "Out."

"Checkmate, this is Checkmate Two. Calcitra Clunis," said Sergeant Major Top Gordon.

"Calcitra Clunis," came the report from Malpractice McCorckel.

And finally Chief Warrant Officer Calvin Culpepper was on the air saying, "This is Checkmate Four. Calcitra Clunis."

Loco Padilla standing with Colonel Falconi and

38

Colonel Kuyen, took a spoonful of pork and beans from a C-ration can. "Sounds like that's all of 'em, sir," he said between bites.

"Right." Falconi handed the handset back to his radio operator. He nodded to Colonel Kuyen. "We're getting there. We just need more time to set up a strong MLR. Then we can concentrate on preparing a defense in depth. After that we start getting mean and going out to find the bastards."

"Yes, Colonel," Kuyen replied. He pointed. "I see the remainder of the Goons are now returning to us."

Archie Dobbs, leading the way, appeared out of the nearby jungle approaching the command post area. He was followed by Blue Richards and Corporal Ngo, with Ky Luyen bringing up the rear. Loco Padilla waved to the arrivals and motioned them to join him in the Goon bivouac area nearby. They would be on call twenty-four hours a day in case any need for their services arose.

Falconi and Kuyen settled down at the roots of a xoai tree. Kuyen chuckled. "Normally I would have my orderly serve tea at this time." Even his personal servant had been relieved of valet duties and sent to one of the assault commandos. "Perhaps I shall acquire some good habits from you, Colonel Falconi."

"There is something I would like to acquire from you, Colonel Kuyen," Falconi said. "Can you give me some information on the NVA troops we are facing out here?"

Kuyen shook his head. "I must apologize, Colonel. I am indeed sorry. We know very little except they are an elite infantry unit."

"You have no idea where their headquarters is? Or supply depots and base camps?"

"No, Colonel Falconi," Kuyen admitted. "All my time in battle with the enemy has been on the defensive. I was never able to afford the luxury of reconnaissance."

"And you got no prisoners?" Falconi inquired.

"No, Colonel. Not even a wounded one. We were in constant retreat," Kuyen said.

Falconi pointed over to where Loco Padilla and his Goon team relaxed. "That's what I've got those apes for. Padilla is a marine, Blue Richards a navy Seal, Ky Luyen a former Viet Cong, and Archie Dobbs is the best damned scout in the whole United States Army. All of them have mean streaks and like to go out and make contact."

"The man I chose for you—Corporal Ngo—is also a fierce and brave soldier," Kuyen said. "He will fit in well with the Goons."

"I strongly believe in aggressive and constant patrolling," Falconi said. "Both for raiding and scouting. It keeps the enemy off balance and damned good and nervous, too. But right now, I'm afraid, we're the ones teetering around here in the jungle. We don't have the slightest idea of the bad guy's strength, location, intent, or—"

An explosion of small arms fire blasted out from the direction of the line of resistance. The Vietnamese radio operator ran up to Falconi and handed him the handset. "You have been raised, *Dai Ta*," he said.

"This is Checkmate," Falconi said.

"Checkmate, this is Checkmate Two," came Top Gordon's voice. "I got what looks like a whole damned NVA battalion slamming straight into us."

"Roger, Checkmate Two," Falconi said. "Maintain your position while I get SITREPS from the other commandos. Over."

"Wilco," Top replied over the radio. "I'll give it a try. Out."

Next Falconi turned his attention to Ray Swift Elk and his First Commando. "Checkmate One. What's your situation? Over."

"We're getting a light probing attack," Swift Elk replied. "No sweat so far. We can hold. Out."

That was good news as far as Falconi was concerned. "Checkmate Three, this is Checkmate. Over."

Master Sergeant Malpractice McCorckel's voice was calm as he answered the request for a SITREP—

situation report. "We're getting slammed pretty hard. I can't assess the exact situation right now. Out."

Falconi glanced at Kuyen. "At this point all we can do is wait and see how the situation develops."

Back in his position up at the front, Malpractice gave the radio handset back to his operator. "I need you to take a quick look up forward," he said to Gunnar Olson. "If it looks bad and you can straighten things up, do it." He tapped their Vietnamese liaison officer on the shoulder. "I would appreciate your help too, Lieutenant Gyo."

"Of course," Gyo said.

Gunnar and the South Vietnamese rushed down to where the ARVN squads were returning the heavy incoming fire. Numerous ranger bodies were scattered around, giving evidence of the ferocity of the surprise attack. Most of them had been caught in the open while digging their positions.

Gunnar turned toward the rear where the commando's weapon squad had been quickly set up. "Machine guns forward!" he ordered.

Lieutenant Gyo repeated the order in Vietnamese. "Sung may! Tien len!"

The young NCO in charge of the machine guns ordered both his crews to pick up their weapons and move toward the front. Sergeant Gunnar Olson simply pointed to a spot where he wanted each gun set up. The well-drilled rangers wasted not one second as they brought their Browning .30 calibers back into action.

"Fire left front!" Gunnar yelled at one. "Right front!" he directed the other.

Both Brownings cranked into action, spewing out the .30 caliber bullets in firebursts of seven to ten rounds. There was a marked slowing down in the enemy attack. By that time, Malpractice had joined his two subordinate commanders.

"How's it going?" he asked in the explosive din of the fighting.

41

"Can't tell yet, Sarge," Gunnar answered. "The bastards weren't expecting that enfilading fire. It knocked 'em off balance."

But the advantage quickly faded away. Pressure from the front built up as more skirmishing NVA troops moved into the attack. The incoming fire grew in intensity, producing more casualties among the rangers.

"First section!" Malpractice yelled. "Lay down covering fire! Second and third move back!" He grabbed Gunnar. "Take charge of the machine guns. Have 'em ease back, but not far enough they can't help us with support fire."

"Gotcha!" Gunnar said rushing off to the task.

"You can help me coordinate this withdrawal," Malpractice yelled at Gyo. "I want to stabilize our line."

"I understand," Gyo said.

Using alternating sections to cover, and with the machine guns joining in, the Third Commando were finally able to break contact long enough to align and adjust their defense. But the NVA were undeterred. They kept coming on.

"Checkmate," radioed Malpractice. "This is Checkmate Three. I got to get the hell outta here! Over!"

"Any retrograde has to be coordinated," Falcni broadcast back. "Your orders are to hang in until you get word from me to do something different. Out."

Things weren't getting any better over in Sergeant Major Top Gordon's Second Commando. The NVA's attack was well coordinated, with covering heavy-weapons fire. They probed forward in heavy columns, almost weaving back and forth across Top's defensive line. The result was that the entire commando had been pushed back into a small, tight formation. ARVN dead were starting to pile up in the hellacious fury of the Reds' relentless salvos.

Steve Matsuno emptied a magazine. He pulled a freshly loaded one from his ammo pouch. "We're gonna be goners in about fifteen more minutes, Top," he said.

42

"I want to move forward," Top said doggedly.

Chief Sergeant Hao was skeptical. "We have much pressure up front. Think can be done?"

"It *has* to be done, goddamnit!" Top said. "Step up the machine gun fire for a full thirty seconds. Then we're going to go straight ahead into the bastards."

On orders, the Brownings' rate of fire was increased to a steady hosing. The tracers flew crazily off into the air as they bounced off trees. Top waited until the sweep hand of his watch indicated that a half minute had passed.

"Forward! Tien len!" the sergeant major bellowed.

The commando surged toward the attackers. More rangers toppled to the ground as they closed with the enemy. But the NVA's fire power and determination were too great. They quickly recovered their equilibrium and renewed their assault. For more than two minutes, Top's men slugged it out toe-to-toe, trading round for round in the roaring hell of the battle. But in the end they were too heavily outnumbered.

Top ordered them back. Then he went back on the communications net. "This is Commando Two. Requesting orders to pull back. Over."

"Checkmate Two, can you hang on a bit longer? Over," Falconi asked over the air.

"We'll do our best," Top replied. "But if we stick around here much longer, there won't be nobody left to order out."

"I understand," Falconi said.

Over on the other flank, Ray Swift Elk and Paulo Garcia, along with their ranger counterpart Captain Huy, weren't having a bad time at all. In fact, things were downright easygoing over in the First Commando.

"There's one hell of a battle going on in the right of the line," Paulo said.

"Yes," Captain Huy said. "I think it best we go forward and give the NVA a good beating."

"My idea exactly," Ray said. "Let's get the men moving."

The First Commando left their still unprepared positions and moved in several skirmish lines into the jungle. They went without any opposition for twenty meters. Suddenly they received some incoming fire that caused two men to be lightly wounded.

"Keep it going!" Swift Elk yelled.

They traveled another fifteen meters, then resistance ahead stiffened somewhat. "Covering fire!" Ray ordered. "Rifle sections, straight ahead!"

They slogged forward and met a more determined effort. The commando finally came to a complete halt in response to shouted orders. A couple of more assaults dwindled under their return fire, forcing the NVA to turn back.

"I'd swear those bastards are giving us just enough to stop us," Paulo Garcia said.

"Then I guess we'll have to show 'em just how stubborn we are," Ray said. He ordered yet another attack.

Back at the command post, Falconi and Colonel Kuyen kept monitoring incoming reports. Off to the side, anxious to give a hand, Loco Padilla and his Goon team waited impatiently. Suddenly Top's voice broke over the radio.

"My situation has turned to pure shit," he reported.

"Hang on, Checkmate Two," Falconi asked of him. He raised Malpractice. "Give me a SITREP, Checkmate Three."

"We're losing it. Out," was the terse reply. "I estimate I got twenty-five percent casualties now."

Then Top was back. "Checkmate, this is Checkmate Two. It looks like the enemy is lightening up. Maybe we can make it. Out."

And Malpractice also had good, unexpected news. "Things are better now. Cancel the request to withdraw. Out."

But the elation that Falconi felt didn't last long. It was dashed to the ground when Ray Swift Elk came over the net. "This is Checkmate One. The situation has exploded in our faces. The enemy has now launched heavy attacks from the right. They're rolling up my flank. Over."

Now Falconi understood what had happened. The NVA hit Top and Malpractice hard to drive them back, while Ray Swift Elk had simply been contained. Now, with the Second and Third commandos driven back, the NVA turned to the separated First Commando and began to rake the unfortunate outfit with heavy fire as they pressed forward. If Ray Swift Elk wasn't helped—and helped fast—he and his men would be massacred before another half hour passed.

Falconi stood up and looked toward the Goons. "Loco! Come over here!"

The marine ran up to his commander. "Yes, sir?"

"Ray is outflanked and he's going to be eaten alive if I don't act quick. There is no choice but to order a full retreat all along the line. So I'm putting you and your guys in it up to your ears," Falconi said. "The rest of the strike force is clearing the hell out of here and consolidating farther back. But I want you and the Goons to stay and go to ground. After the NVA move in here and set up, I want you to come out of cover and work your way through the lines and rejoin us."

"A stay-behind operation, huh, sir?" Loco asked.

"Exactly," Falconi replied. "And I'll expect a full recon during your exfiltration through the enemy unit."

"Yes, sir!" Loco said.

"Go for it and good luck," Falconi said.

The marine quickly ran back to the Goon Team and gave them a rundown on the perilous task assigned to them. "The old man said we'd be up to our ears," Loco told the team.

Archie Dobbs snorted. "Up to our ears, hell! We'll be over our heads in boiling shit!"

Chapter 5

For an hour or so after the enemy moved into the area, Loco Padilla gave the matter of staying behind some quick but serious thought. It was dangerous as hell, and a situation that presented several options for him to consider. But no matter which one the marine NCO chose, it stood a good chance of proving to be wrong—fatally wrong . . .

"This," Loco said to himself, "is what they mean when they say you're between the rock and the hard place."

If the enemy discovered them soon after sweeping into the area, the NVA troops would massacre the Goons in the heat of battle craziness. However, if a bit of time passed and the combatants had settled down somewhat and lost some of the initial rage built up by the fighting, they would probably not shoot them out of hand. Instead, there would be a quick and brutal field interrogation. After that, the survivors could look forward to months or even years of captivity.

Either way, the Goons were between that rock and hard place. A wrong move or decision would be disastrous.

After a quick explanation of their mission to the team, Loco led them back toward the rear. "We need to find some concealment," he told them. "We gotta do it quick and make the right choice, too. We don't want some

46

numb-fuck NVA just stumbling across us any more'n we need some hotshot digging us out by pulling off a thorough recon."

After the Goons had moved almost fifty meters, they finally discovered a grove of khoai-sap plants. This vegetation, growing to seven or eight feet in height, had large leaves that could cause painful blistering of the mouth and tongue if they were eaten. That was one reason Loco made the command decision to hide among them. Any Vietnamese in his right mind would regard khoai-sap with about the same abhorrence that Americans felt for poison ivy or poison oak.

"Here's our home away from home," he announced. The marine gently parted a couple of the large leaves to avoid breaking them. Damaged plants could also attract the attention of some quick-witted enemy trooper.

A quick look satisfied him. "Okay. In you go, boys."

Blue Richards eased into the grove, also taking care not to cause any damage to the plant. He was quickly followed by Archie, the ARVN ranger Corporal Trang Ngo, and Ky Luyen. Ky was encumbered by the radio, yet he managed the task with the ease of a practiced soldier in good physical condition.

Each Goon showed the same concern for the vegetation as Loco and Blue. This wasn't because of any devotion to conservation. In order to have their concealment go undetected, it was terribly important to make the area appear completely undisturbed. After Ky went inside, Loco followed. He stopped long enough to lean out and brush away any telltale bootprints. After rearranging the leaves, he joined the others to wait out the inevitable arrival of the enemy.

The battle suddenly flared up even more. If Falconi was going to make a safe withdrawal, he would have to make it at that moment. Loco reached over and grabbed the handset of the AN/PRC-77. "Checkmate, this is Checkmate Five. We are in position. Over." Loco found it difficult to hear Falconi's voice over the radio when

47

he replied.

The colonel said, "Hang tight, Checkmate Five. We're pulling out after one quick counterattack. Things are going to get hairy, so stay close to mother earth. Over."

"This is Checkmate Five. Wilco and out," Loco said. He returned the handset to its place on the radio. "Keep low, guys. We're about to become orphans in the forest."

The sounds of the fighting suddenly increased even more. They heard some grenades going off in the distance. All the Black Eagles in the khoai-sap grove recognized Falconi's favorite way of breaking contact before hauling ass. A few well-tossed grenades always took out some bad guys and it made their buddies duck and become more respectful.

Now the battle rolled toward them and the Goons heard the sound of running feet. These sounds stopped now and again as the withdrawing men turned and delivered covering fire for their buddies farther up front. After a few sharp salvos—and some more grenades—the retreat continued.

A brief lull followed; the sudden silence in the jungle seemed like an alien condition.

Archie chuckled. "The old man done a good job. He's managed to put some space between our guys and the NVA."

Blue nodded. "Yeah. Which means they'll be right up here right quick now."

"It also means to shut the fuck up!" Loco growled.

The Goons followed the team leader's undiplomatic order. In a short five minutes they could hear the first NVA skirmishers approaching. The Reds, reconnoitering by firepower, sprayed intermittent swarms of 7.63-millimeter slugs ahead of them as they moved in. A few smacked the leaves of the grove concealing the Goons. They instinctively pushed their faces into the dirt.

Soon they heard voices of the North Vietnamese officers and non-com squad leaders directing their men during the slow advance:

"Tien len!"

"Durng thanh hang!"

"Di cham loi!"

Occasionally the leaves of the Goons' hiding place shook as troops walked close enough to brush against them. But Loco's idea that they would have a natural inclination to stay away proved correct. None of the passing enemy soldiers suspected that anyone would use the grove for concealment. After fifteen minutes the area grew quieter. Soon there was silence.

Loco clicked his tongue to get Archie's attention. He signaled him to take a look. Archie nodded and slowly crawled to the edge of the large leaves. He peered through them for a full five minutes before pulling back. "They've gone by," he whispered.

"Right," Loco said. "Let's settle in and wait."

For a long time the surrounding rain forest was quiet. Not even animals or insects made a sound. The effect of the day's fighting had frightened the natural denizens of the area away. Only a few buzzing insects remained.

"Listen!" Blue said under his breath.

Five pairs of ears strained until they finally all perceived the distant sounds of digging and chopping. Loco grinned. "That's it. The son of a bitches are settling in." He reached for the radio. "Checkmate, this is Checkmate Five," he said into the transmitter. His voice was only loud enough to be able to communicate through the instrument.

Because the volume had been turned down, Falconi's voice was hard to pick up even in the receiver. "This is Checkmate. Over."

"The enemy has ceased advancing," Loco informed him. "They're digging in and setting up a Mike Lima Romeo. Over."

"Roger," Falconi said. "Don't begin your exfiltration until just before dawn. Our outposts will be alerted for you. Over."

"Roger. Out," Loco said. He turned the radio back to

Ky. "Okay, boys. We'll settle in for the night with one guy on guard at all times. Blue, take the first watch. Ky the second, Ngo the third, and I'll stand the last. Try to get some sleep. Early tomorrow we're gonna take a stroll through that NVA battalion."

"Thanks so much for reminding me," Archie said. "I'm sure that bit of cheerful news will help me sleep even better."

Loco grinned. "Won't it be exciting?"

Nobody grinned back. Blue Richards, starting his stint of guard duty, moved to the best place to both see and hear what went on outside their hiding place. Everyone else settled in to get some sleep before his own turn as sentry came up.

The night in that isolated concealment passed slowly. The routine of changing reliefs happened quickly and quietly every two hours. When a goon was awakened for guard duty, the man doing the waking up was ready to smother any instinctive mumbling or loud yawns.

Loco didn't allow himself to fall into a deep sleep. He merely dozed and was aware each time the guard changed. As soon as it was evident the new sentry was in place, Loco again dozed off into a shallow, fitful slumber. But when Trang Ngo went on post, Loco finally gave in and went to sleep. There would be only two hours before he was awakened, and he wanted to have some solid rest before he was awakened to take the last watch.

When Ngo finally tapped him lightly on the shoulder, Loco came straight awake. "That time, eh?"

Trang Ngo nodded in the deep darkness and spoke softly. "Two hour to go," he said. "Then rang dong—dawn come after that."

"Okay, Trang," Loco said. "Thanks for the wake-up call. Now get some shuteye."

"Duoc roi," the ranger said.

Loco carefully crawled to the lookout spot and settled in. He turned his head in the direction of the North Vietnamese unit and listened. There wasn't a sound. That was the sign of a highly disciplined outfit. It was going to take a hell of a lot of fighting to defeat them—if the job could be done. But the Black Eagles would have to find out exactly what they were facing. That was the job the Goons would have to perform in the early predawn hours.

The marine thought about all the times he had been on guard duty in the eleven years he'd been in the Corps. At first there had been the stylized walking of posts at boot camp. This was more for training and instilling the seriousness of the job than actually keeping anything secure. Then, later on, at Camp Lejeune and in Okinawa, the guards were really taking care of government property and lives. In Okinawa, they'd walked their posts with a full load of ammo in their M16s. Finally, in Vietnam, a real enemy bent on dealing death and destruction was present. That was when being a guard kept the old adrenalin pumping. Exactly like now, in this goddamned patch of khoai-sap.

Loco stayed alert right up to the time he could first discern the pink coloring of dawn in the east. He turned and moved quietly from man to man, gently shaking them. "Wake up," he whispered. "Rise and shine, boys. We're gonna stroll through one of Uncle Ho's outfits."

The others were quickly awake. Using the fewest movements possible to keep the noise down, they donned their patrol harnesses and secured their weapons.

"Archie, take the point," Loco said. "Blue, cover the rear. Trang, go right—ben phai, understand?"

"Okay," Trang Ngo said cheerfully.

"I'll take the left and Ky the center," Loco said. "Is everybody ready? Okay. Move out."

Their team had assumed a diamond formation. It was a perfect one when a small group didn't know from which side the shit was going to be heaved at them. Archie led them from the koai-sap grove and took the first dangerous steps toward the enemy unit.

Archie set the pace to be slow and deliberate. They had to move through the area before full daylight, but they couldn't make too much speed or the result would be

51

unnecessary noise. Archie's entire being tingled with anticipation and alertness. The natural nervousness he felt made all his senses acutely alert.

Although the flicker of light flashed but a millisecond, Archie saw it.

He signaled for a halt and motioned Loco forward to him. When the team leader arrived, Archie put his lips close to Loco's ear and whispered, "NVA fuckup ahead. Some guard lit a cigarette."

Loco nodded. "Them bastards are full of self-confidence. Sometimes that makes even the best troops careless. Go on around him."

"You don't want to take him out?"

"You know the old man's orders," Loco said. "We're strictly recon unless we have to fight."

"Right," Archie said. "C'mon then."

They traveled another ten minutes without incident until Archie stopped again. Once more Loco went forward. "What's happening?"

"Two NVA ahead," Archie said. "We gotta do a job on 'em."

"Yeah," Loco agreed, surveying the terrain. "We'd never get around 'em." He quietly pulled off his patrol harness and lowered it to the ground. "You and me, babe."

"Right," Archie said imitating him.

Both Black Eagles silently approached two North Vietnamese riflemen. The pair, guarding a stack of supplies, gazed sleepily through the predawn gloom in the direction of their MLR.

Archie and Loco struck simultaneously. Hands clamped over mouths to stifle screams at the exact moment that the cold steel of their knives sliced into the lower backs just under the rib cage. Their victims instinctively tried to jump away as the blades were brutally forced upward into vital organs. After only a few seconds of struggling the dying shudders of the enemy soldiers announced the end of their lives.

After gently lowering the cadavers to the ground, they returned to the others and slipped back into their gear. A quick signal from Archie to follow, and the patrol continued.

As they moved along, each man caught short glimpses of the enemy position. As practiced soldiers, that was enough to give them plenty of information on the NVA unit they faced.

Finally the small patrol reached the main bivouac. Archie paused long enough to get his bearings and figure out exactly what was ahead of them. He could see numerous hootches made of limbs scattered through the area. Well camouflaged, they would have been impossible to sight from an aircraft.

Archie finally figured what direction he wanted to go. He led the Goons along the edge of the area. As the Black Eagles quietly slid by, they could hear an occasional snore or sleepy murmur. One of the NVA emitted a loud fart in his sleep. Archie grinned, thinking all soldiers were the same.

As they neared the enemy main line of resistance, the scout spotted a swamp. It would make a good place to exit and enter no man's land between the opposing forces.

It took two full hours to make their way through the thick, muddy water. Each step was a strained effort in the murky depth that ranged from knee high to up to their armpits.

Finally they emerged onto dryer land. Loco signaled a halt. "Ky, bring the radio here."

Ky walked over and squatted down beside the team leader. "We learn a lot, eh?"

"Damn right we did," Loco said getting the handset from its place. "Checkmate," he transmitted. "This is Checkmate Five. Alert the outposts. We're coming in and we got good intel. Over."

Falconi's voice sounded good when he said, "We're waiting for you, Checkmate Five. Come on in and welcome back home."

53

Chapter 6

Colonel Robert Falconi and Colonel Long Kuyen both listened as Staff Sergeant Loco Padilla made his report at their rustic command post.

"We're facing a reinforced infantry battalion," Loco informed them. "There's a small headquarters detachment that don't amount to shit. They just seem to be there to coordinate what the commander wants as quick as they can. From the way things run, I'd say those boys don't believe in too much administration."

Falconi smiled sardonically. "I wish I could say the same for the U.S. Army. At any rate, how many rifle companies do you estimate we're facing?" the colonel asked.

"Four, sir," Loco replied. "That ain't unusual, but they got extra squads in their platoons."

"The NVA commander evidently wants to keep unit integrity at a maximum," Falconi remarked.

"Yes, sir," Loco said. "They've been organized to do more than just slug it out. Them dudes is storm troopers in the purest sense of the word."

"As we so well know," Colonel Kuyen said. "What is their heavy weaponry?"

"They got some real bad shit. We seen ammo crates for mortars—Soviet M1937s," Loco said.

"82-millimeter," Falconi remarked. "Great big heavy bastards."

"And that ain't all," Loco said. "They had some Chicom Type 36 recoilless rifles, too. 57-millimeter babies they were. There didn't seem to be too many of 'em, but you can shoot out a gnat's eye at five hundred meters with one o' them."

"Son of a bitch!" Falconi exclaimed.

"I ain't finished, sir," Loco went on. "We also seen some DShK heavy machine guns. They're big bastards. 12.7-millimeter babies that can be tipped up for anti-aircraft work."

"If they have all that heavy weaponry, why have they not deployed it?" Colonel Long Kuyen wanted to know.

"They're being economical for a couple of reasons I can think of," Falconi said grimly. "The first reason is that they haven't had to use it. Those reinforced rifle platoons have been real ass-kickers. And the second is obvious. They want to keep their true numbers in weaponry and personnel strength under wraps until they absolutely have to reveal it."

"That is one big bad bunch of mothers we're facing, sir," Loco added. "We really noticed their discipline. There wasn't a peep out of 'em all through the night. The only thing we seen was when one fuckup lit a cigarette."

"Every outfit has one," Falconi said.

"They sure do. But I got to tell you, sir, this here operation ain't gonna be no picnic."

"You'll get no argument from me on that point," Falconi said. "Show me their positions on the map."

Loco traced across the printed topographic features with his finger. "The enemy MLR runs down through here, see? The right flank is well covered by the heavy stuff. Over here on the left, the NVA commander has anchored his left flank to a swamp. We used it to get out."

"How was it for your patrol to move through?" Colonel Kuyen asked.

"Shitty, sir," Loco answered. "It was tough enough for my little team to get through it. You ain't gonna take a large unit and do much in that swamp."

"I have been there once myself with a patrol," Colonel Kuyen said. "Any large unit that enters there will be mired down in a short period of time. It would make them—how you Americans so colorfully say?—sitting ducks."

"That's exactly why the North Vietnamese are using it to protect them on that side of the line," Falconi said.

"We need reinforcements," Kuyen said. "Alas, my own forces cannot supply any. I had hopes the American command would be able to send us more men."

Falconi shook his head. "If the U.S. brass had people available that they could spare for this part of the war, they would have sent a whole damned infantry battalion instead of our detachment."

"We're all you get, sir," Loco said to the South Vietnamese ranger officer.

"Then we must fight harder," Kuyen said.

"You sound like a man who is ready to kick ass," Falconi said.

"I am a man who is tired of getting *his* ass kicked," Kuyen said sullenly.

"That is the meanest kind of dude there is," Loco said. "A fed-up guy is real dangerous to deal with." He grinned. "That's why I don't never mess with nobody else's old lady."

"You bet," Falconi replied. "Good morals and behavior be damned. It's best to avoid getting done in by a jealous lover, right?"

"Right," Loco said.

"Thanks for the report, Loco. Now you get some sleep and tell your men to do the same. I'm certain I'll have some more shit details for you Goons."

"Just let us know, sir," Loco said giving a salute.

"I'm going to radio back and tell that damned Fagin to go to General Taggart. I want those headquarters types to prepare some sort of support for us," Falconi said. "Then we're going to launch the goddamndest attack those

56

North Vietnamese bastards have ever experienced."

"The NVA will bring their heavy weapons into the fight then, Colonel," Long Kuyen pointed out.

"And it will bring the final showdown closer," Falconi said. "This is a situation where there won't be a draw, Colonel Kuyen. Either we're going to win and kill all those sons of bitches, or they'll do the same to us." He signaled to the waiting radio operator.

The young ARVN soldier trotted over holding out the handset for the American colonel.

Andrea Thuy's fingers danced across the typewriter keyboard, putting the final touches on the after-action report of the Black Eagles' entrance into Operation Bo-Binh. She had just pulled the paper from the roller when the door of her office opened.

An armed MP stuck his head in. "Howdy, Lieutenant Thuy," he said to her.

Andrea smiled. "Hello, Sergeant. What brings you around this time of day?"

"I'm an escort," the soldier explained. "I've got three guys with me. Okay for 'em to come in?"

"Sure. We're expecting visitors," Andrea said.

The soldier pulled his head back. Andrea could hear his voice as he said, "Pass through, gentlemen. The lady says you're welcome."

Tim Donegan, Choy Chieu, and Mike McKeever walked in. Choy and McKeever went over and sat down on the settee across the room. Donegan stood in front of Andrea's desk. "We got word that Fagin wants to see us."

"He sure does," Andrea said.

"Hello, Andrea," Choy called out.

"Hullo," McKeever said.

"How are you guys doing?" Andrea asked.

"We're kind of excited," Donegan said. "Our case officer has said we been transferred to Fagin."

"They put us in isolation," McKeever said in his deep

57

ponderous voice. "They won't let us go nowheres a'tall wit'out thére be a MP watchin' us."

"Those are the rules," Andrea said. "At any rate, you all look in fine fettle."

Choy rubbed his hands together. "We are ready for action, you betcha!"

Andrea smiled and stood up. "You're probably going to get it too," she said. She went to Chuck Fagin's door and rapped on it. After pushing it open, she beckoned the three flyers to enter.

Fagin was all smiles when he greeted them. "Hi ya, boys. C'mon in and make yourselves at home. By God! It's really good to see you."

"Do you got'ny Guinness Stout?" McKeever asked, looking at Fagin's wet bar in the corner of his office.

"No, I ain't, boys," Fagin said. "Damn! If I'd known I was gonna be calling you three over, I'd have made sure there was some on hand. But I just got word on this new situation a short time ago. Hell, I even said to Andrea just a minute ago, 'Damn! I wish I had some Guinness Stout for Donegan, Choy, and McKeever.'" He looked over at Andrea standing in the door. "Didn't I say that, Andrea?"

"You sure did," Andrea said. "I have some more work to do. If you need me, I'll be at my desk."

Andrea left and Fagin, after more profuse apologies about the dearth of Guinness Stout, invited the trio to help themselves to what ever they wanted in his bar.

All three fetched themselves beer. Donegan and Choy got a can apiece, but McKeever got an entire six pack. They popped the cans of suds and settled down on the battered sofa across from Fagin's desk. Donegan took a deep sip of beer then asked, "So what's going on, Chuck? How's come you sent for us?"

"How would you guys like to give Falconi and his boys a bit of aerial support?" Fagin asked.

"Sure," Choy said.

"I told him we didn't have much to do," Donegan said.

58

"We'll be happy to lend them guys a hand."

"That's great, boys," Fagin said. "A radio message came in from Falconi requesting air attack support. And there's nothing available right now but the PBY. But at least the air force can give us some logistic support on the mission."

"Jesus!" Donegan said. "Our bird is a transport aircraft, mainly. And it ain't the fastest bird in the sky, neither. Why, hell, the only weaponry we have are the .50-caliber machine guns."

McKeever belched. "We got bomb racks, ain't we?"

"Very true," Choy chimed in. "But they are no good for missiles. Only bombs."

"That's prob'ly why they call 'em bomb racks," McKeever mused. He tossed an empty can over the bar and opened a fresh one.

They were interrupted by a knock on the door. Andrea stuck her pretty face in. "That air force ordnance officer has arrived, Chuck."

"Great!" Fagin said. "Send him in."

Andrea opened the door and a major stepped into the room. He seemed a cheerful sort. "How do you do, Mister Fagin. I'm Major Reynolds. My boss over at Area Ordnance gave me the word to come see you." He laughed. "This Hai-Cat is a nice place, but the security is murder!"

"That's the nature of the business. But I'm certainly glad to know you, Major," Fagin said. He introduced Donegan, Choy, and McKeever. "Care for a drink?"

"No, thank you," Reynolds said. "As our colleagues in the navy say, 'The sun isn't over the yardarm yet.'" He chuckled. "I'm real anxious to get something cleared up before we get down to business, though."

"Sure," Fagin said.

"Somebody really screwed up the information I received," the major said. "I heard you people were planning on using a PBY for ground-support operations."

59

"We are," Fagin said.

"It's actually a PBY-5A amphibian," Donegan said.

Reynolds stared at them. "You're fucking kidding me."

McKeever shook his head. "We ain't fucking kidding. It's a PBY-5A awright."

"No, no," Reynolds said. "I mean you're kidding you are going to use it for a ground-support attack aircraft."

"That is exactly what we're going to do," Fagin said.

"I think I will have a drink," Reynolds said. He went to the bar and fixed a scotch on the rocks. "You can't fire missiles from that aircraft, can you?" he asked turning back to the men.

"No," Choy said.

"We got bomb racks," McKeever said. "Give us some bombs, okay?"

"You want bombs for a close-in ground-support operation?" Reynolds asked. "What about other armament?"

"We need .50 ball and tracer for the machine guns," Donegan said. "We got one for'd, one aft, and two amidships."

"Look, fellows," Reynolds said. He spoke as if he were addressing slobbering lunatics. "The only kind of bomb I can get you for that particular aircraft is the free-fall type. You'll have to release them from two thousand feet in order to give them time to arm themselves before striking the ground. Do you have a bombsight?"

"No," Choy answered.

"Then you'll have to dive bomb for accuracy," Reynolds said. "In a PBY!"

But Donegan shook his head. He pointed to Choy. "This here navigator is a mathematical genius. He can figger out trajectories, wind drift, and altitude adjustments as easy as McKeever here can piss in a pot."

"Easier!" Choy chimed in.

"Jesus!" Reynolds exclaimed. "If you make any sort of error in calculation you will either miss or fly into your own bomb blast. Don't you even have a cannon?"

60

"Nope," Donegan said. "Just the .50 calibers."

The Air Force officer sighed. "Okay. I'll get the bombs on requisition and out here to you right away. The same for the machine gun ammo. And I think I'll make it all tracer. It'll help your aim. You're going to need all the advantages you can possibly get."

"That's very nice o' you," McKeever said.

"Is there anything else?" Reynolds asked.

"That's it," Fagin answered. "We certainly thank you very much."

Reynolds walked to the door and opened. He hesitated, then turned around with a serious expression on his face. "You guys are fucking crazy!"

Loco Padilla led the quartet of Goons up to the command post. They had all enjoyed a good nap. Now, feeling rested, they answered this summons from the commanding officer with enthusiasm.

"Something tells me you got a job for the Goon Team, sir," Loco said.

"I sure as hell do," Falconi answered. "You guys did a good reconnaissance job coming back through the lines. But we need a bit more information to complete the picture."

"You bet, sir," Archie Dobbs said.

"What's going on?" Blue Richards asked.

"I've asked for air support for the next attack," Falconi explained. "That means they'll probably send us some F-4 Phantom jets for the close-in work. I haven't received any confirmation on that, but it seems the logical conclusion for an operation like this."

Ky Luyen grinned. "We need to find targets. Right, Colonel?"

"We do it for you," Corporal Trang Ngo added.

"You guys have a good attitude," Falconi said.

"You bet, sir," Loco said. "We'll locate some juicy places to blow the hell out of. C'mon, guys, let's saddle up and get this show on the road."

"Hold it," Falconi said. "There is one more thing. Just one more itty-bitty thing that needs tending to."

"Uh oh!" Archie exclaimed.

Loco eyed the detachment commander. "What is this here one more *itty-bitty* thing, sir?"

"We need a prisoner," Falconi said.

"Sure," Loco said. "We can get you one, sir."

"He has to be an officer," Falconi added.

Blue smiled a bit. "That adds a bit to it, sir."

"Not just any type of officer," Falconi went on. "He has to be a staff officer."

Archie grinned. "You want a left-handed one or a right-handed one?"

Falconi gave the matter some thought. Finally he said, "Oh, hell, I guess it doesn't make any difference. Either one will be fine."

"Oh, thank you, sir," Archie said rolling his eyes. "You're really a softy at heart, ain't you?"

Falconi smiled. "It's just that I'm so crazy about you guys."

Chapter 7

The Goons got down to the bare essentials for the demanding job Colonel Robert Falconi had given them.

They tied olive-drab scarfs around their heads in place of helmets or caps; jacket and trouser cuffs were taped down to keep them from being caught in the brush; the Goons removed the slings from their M16s and stripped their pistol belts of everything except two ammo pouches, canteen, and knife. Following those chores, the patrol colored their faces with streaks of black and dark green camouflage paint and removed their dogtags. To make sure there would be no other evidence of their identities, wallets or personal possessions were removed from their pockets.

Other soldiers captured by the enemy might be allowed to reveal their names, dates of birth, and service numbers, but in clandestine outfits like the Black Eagles, even that small amount of information was enough to cause serious compromise of intelligence information. There was also the insidious potential for situations such as blackmail or threats to families back in the States.

When they were finally ready for their patrol, Loco Padilla made a simple but effective inspection of each man. He started out with Archie Dobbs. "Jump up and down," Loco instructed him.

Archie hopped around.

"Good," Loco said. He pointed to Ky Luyen. The ex-Viet Cong did likewise, as did the tough Corporal Trang Ngo of the ARVN rangers.

When Blue Richards jumped, something jangled. His face reddened with embarrassment and he reached in his pocket bringing out a couple of coins. "Dang! I forgot about these."

"Carelessness like that can kill folks," Loco said coldly. "Watch it in the future."

"You bet," Blue said. "I'm real sorry." He felt like a basic trainee caught with unshined boots. The navy Seal handed the dime and quarter over to Gunnar Olson, who was nearby watching the Goons get ready for their foray behind enemy lines.

"Hot damn!" Gunnar said. "I made thirty-five cents and I was just standing here."

"I want that cash back," Blue said.

"You two take care of them big finances tomorrow," Loco said. "All Goons gather 'round and I'll give you a rundown on this here patrol."

The men in the team squatted down in front of the marine sergeant.

"We're going back in through that same swamp we come out of," Loco said.

"Yuk!" Archie complained. "That place is one of the worst I ever been in."

"Just remember that we're as safe in there as a baby in his mama's arms," Blue pointed out.

"We'll discuss the particular features of that swamp *after* the patrol," Loco said. "Now listen up. From there we'll move north of the enemy MLR, and I want ever'-body to take special note of not only *what* we see but *where* we see it, so's I can mark it on the map for Colonel Falconi. This is real important, 'cause he needs this info to direct the air force hot shots that will be flying support missions for us. The only way we'll be able to knock off them NVA heavy weapons is with strike missions."

"Shit!" Ky Luyen said. "We go get them ourselves."

"Sure!" Corporal Trang Ngo agreed. "More fun, kong co?"

"You two bastards is crazy," Loco said. "I prefer to let the flyboys do that kind of dirty work."

Archie held up his hand. "I think we also should check out some obvious places where it looks like we could break through in a ground attack. There's got to be someplace in that goddamned NVA battalion where their shit is weak."

"We can look," Loco said. "But we won't find any, I'll bet. The guy commanding that bunch don't pull punches. He's a badass that's squared away and mean."

"Maybe so. But if we find their headquarters, that'll help," Blue said.

"I hope like hell we can find their headquarters," Loco said. "Because that's exactly where I want to go to get our prisoner."

Ky Luyen laughed. "Falconi no joke when he say he want staff officer, huh?"

Corporal Ngo shook his head. "I think Colonel Falconi maybe never joke."

"You're right," Loco said. "So ever'body remember. We're going to mark locations and get a prisoner that can fill in intelligence on what we miss. When those big Phantom jets come roaring in here, we want to give them the best goddamned targets we can."

"Amen!" Archie said.

"Okay, here's our formation," Loco continued. "Archie takes the point as usual. Ky, you follow him. I'll come after Ky with Trang behind me."

"Well," Blue said lazily. "It looks like I'm the tail on this ol' dawg."

"That you are," Loco said. "Okay. On your feet. Lock and load, then slip on your safeties. Quickly!" He waited for the men to ready their weapons. "Okay, Goons. Move it out!"

The small column walked up to the front lines in the gloom of early evening. The ARVN rangers who were members of Malpractice's Third Commando watched dully as the patrol walked quietly through their dug-in positions.

Less than fifty meters past the line, Archie's boots hit the soft, dank earth that marked the beginning of the swamp. Another twenty minutes and the patrol reached the water. They all instinctively grimaced as they penetrated farther into the muddy, stinking water.

Archie spat, saying to himself, "This is like going through a big unflushed toilet, for Chrissake!"

As he led the Goons on, the water deepened from their ankles up to their knees. After awhile they were chest deep in the fetid liquid. Archie was startled on numerous occasions by sudden splashes in the water. It made him wonder what sort of animals or reptiles were close by. The thought of snakes around made him shudder involuntarily. There were two things that Archie Dobbs hated—a closed bar and snakes.

Finally the depth of the water receded bit by bit until the patrol slogged through ankle-deep sludge. Another fifty meters and the ground grew firmer. Then, two hours after their odyssey into danger began, the Goons emerged from the swamp and into the jungle.

"This," Loco whispered to his men, "is bandit country."

Archie turned for directions. Loco pointed to the northwest. Nodding, the point man stepped off along that compass line. Now the pace really slowed. The Goons walked carefully on a route that took them straight into the heart of the enemy. They knew that NVA units were all around them and that the chances of stumbling across the Reds had increased a hundredfold since coming out of that stinking swamp.

Archie suddenly ducked down.

The patrol, as veterans will do, also hit the dirt. This wasn't done with a careless dive to terra firma. The Goons squatted first, then quietly lay down to avoid rustling the brush around them. After half a minute,

Loco slowly crawled forward and joined the scout.

"What's up?" he asked in a whisper.

"Heavy machine gun section," Archie replied just as softly. "Over there. See 'em?"

"Yeah," Loco said peering with the scout through the brush. "Looks like they're getting ready to clean their guns."

The North Vietnamese soldiers were quick and efficient. Only one of the Russian 12.7-millimeter DShK guns was dismounted at a time.

"They know what they're doing," Loco said with approval.

"Yeah," Archie agreed. "They only take one weapon at a time out of operation. If they're attacked, they still got the other three ready and standing by for action."

As soon as the first gun was cleaned and oiled, it was reassembled. Then another was taken down for its turn at preventive maintenance.

"We're up against some real sharp bastards," Loco said.

"This is gonna be a hell of a tough operation, all right," Archie allowed. A movement off to one side caught his eye. "Ammo detail coming up."

Several pairs of troopers, each team carrying a litter loaded with ammunition boxes, came out of the jungle. Without speaking they dropped their burdens, distributing the small crates of bullets around the guns. When the task was completed, they wordlessly and quickly withdrew.

"Damn!" Loco said observing the simplicity of the NVA delivery system—fluid, adaptable, and uncomplicated. "And the son of a bitches are well supplied, too." He pulled out his map and studied it. "I ain't got 'em marked down. We must've missed that bunch on our exfiltration."

"That's why Falconi wants us to snatch a staff officer," Archie said. "He can fill in any gaps we leave."

"Right. Okay, let's move on."

Hand and arm signals were given to the rest of the patrol, then Archie resumed leading them into the enemy's hinterlands. In only fifteen minutes he found another heavy weapons outfit. This time it was a mortar section.

"Damn!" Loco said under his breath as he looked at the M1937s manned by the NVA. "Is this one we seen before that moved, or is it a new outfit?"

"We probably seen 'em before," Archie said.

"The crux o' the NVA defense is them mortars. I really gotta get an accurate map marking," Loco said. He snapped his fingers at Blue.

The navy Seal crawled forward, joining them. "What's happening?"

"I need a resection to get these bastards exactly pinpointed," Loco said. "I want them jets to make sure-fire hits on 'em."

"The only way we're gonna do that is have someone climb a tree and shoot some azimuths," Blue remarked.

"Why the hell do you think I called you over here?" Loco asked. Blue was the best tree climber in the Black Eagles.

"I'm flattered," Blue said.

"Just get you ass up high and do the job," Loco said.

"Right," Blue said. He looked around and noted a tamarind tree. "There's just what the ol' doctor ordered." The Alabamian pulled off his pistol belt and left his rifle behind. Then he shimmied up almost seventy-five feet. When he reached the top, he looked for a couple of prominent terrain features he could identify on the map. He easily picked out a hill and a small lake shimmering off in the near distance. Blue took his compass and sighted it on both places, noting the azimuth reading. It was difficult getting his map arranged up in the tree so it could be oriented, but he managed. By the time he came down and rejoined the patrol on the ground, he had drawn two lines to make the resection.

Where they came together was the mortars' exact location.

"Nice going," Loco said. "How's it look up there?"

"I can't see nothing on the ground," Blue said. "But on the other hand, nobody on the ground can see me, neither."

"Upstairs just might be a good place to hide," Loco said. "Okay. Let's move it on. We got lots to see and do, children."

It took the Goons only five minutes to reach their next discovery. This time it was a rifle company's position. Loco checked his map and noted that they had scouted the unit during their exfiltration. But he decided to observe the enemy for a while to see if anything more could be learned.

They noted that all the enemy troops spoke softly, even whispering in that area that, as far as they knew, was perfectly secure. All fighting positions, including the company command post, were well camouflaged. Even the field latrines had camo material over the top. While the observation went on, a work detail of NVA came out of the jungle with fresh cut vegetation. They replaced older material that was beginning to fade to a different color as it died.

"They don't even give it a chance to turn brown," Archie remarked.

"Right," Loco said. "There ain't any chance of aerial photos showing any change at all. These boys are invisible from the air."

Archie grinned and pointed to where they were marked on the patrol leader's map. "Not no more they ain't."

"I guess not," Loco said. "C'mon. Let's do like the old shepherd and get the flock outta here."

It took three hours of slow patrolling, observing, and map making to reach the farthest end of the NVA lines. More observations and map markings were made on the way before they finally reached the MLR limits. There they found an extremely dense concentration of heavy weaponry set up in a defensive posture. Numerous NVA patrols came and went, but fortunately for the Goons, this activity was going away—not toward them.

"The NVA ain't gonna get outflanked on this end," Loco observed.

Blue, who had done another resection, was situated between Archie and Loco. "If we want to whup 'em, we'll have to hit them bastards straight on and slug it out."

"Don't forget we'll have Phantom jets flying aerial support," Loco reminded him.

"Anything less ain't gonna do," Blue flatly stated.

"There ain't nothing else to see," Archie said. "What's next on our exciting agenda?"

"It's time to get that damn pris'ner," Loco said. "Let's see to that little chore."

"Any ideas where to go?" Archie asked.

"I don't see that we got a lot of choice," Loco said. "If the colonel wants a staff officer, we got to go where the NVA headquarters is. Their battalion CP has got to be farther in the rear to make command and control easier." He nudged Archie. "Take us another fifty meters back, then we'll travel parallel to the MLR 'til we run into something."

"Or someone," Blue added.

Archie followed the orders with his usual precision. After a fifty-meter walk he turned back in the direction of the swamp. The trek through the rear positions proved beneficial as well. Numerous small but well-stocked supply depots were duly marked on the map. The NVA commander kept things scattered and hidden, so that even his rear echelon would be tough to mop up.

The Goons also found a large, wide-open area. It was one of those freaks of nature. Right in the middle of a thick, almost impenetrable jungle, that lush meadow, heavy with thick grass, rolled lazily out in an expanse of two hundred by fifty meters.

"Dang my eyes!" Blue exclaimed. "You could graze a big ol' herd o' cows out there."

"It ain't on the map either," Loco complained. "How the hell do they expect us to fight a real war when the goddamned charts don't tell us ever'thing?"

Archie shrugged. "Nobody ever said that Southeast Asia has been given a complete topographic treatment. It kinda makes you feel like an explorer, don't it?"

"I feel like a tired, old, worn-out leatherneck," Loco said, wiping at the sweat on his face.

"You look like one, too," Archie said matter-of-factly. "What do I look like?"

"You look like you was the only one at an ax fight without an ax," Blue said.

"Goddamn it!" Loco hissed under his breath. "Here we are, way out in the middle of nowhere, smack in the middle of a whole enemy battalion of some of the worstest badasses that Uncle Ho ever sent down his trail, and you two dickheads is carrying on like a couple of schoolboys."

"We'd look a hell of a lot worse if it wasn't for Falconi's physical training sessions in the afternoons," Archie said. "Anyhow, me and Blue are just enjoying ourselves with good old-fashioned American humor."

"Get your ass in gear," Loco growled.

Archie wisely got back to work. He skirted the southern boundary of the meadow, then plunged back into the jungle. After more traveling through the dense brush, they came across what seemed to be a command post.

Although the headquarters area was crude, several large hootches could be seen. Men in the area with mapboards seemed to be involved in various meetings or conferences. The group also sported haversacks containing papers and pencils.

"Them is staff officers, all right!" Archie said happily.

"We'll take one of 'em," Loco said.

"Any ideas?" Blue asked. He, Ky Luyen, and Trang

Ngo had joined the other two.

"Looks like a latrine over there," Loco said. "That's the place."

They pulled back into the rain forest, skirting the camp until they reached their target. Loco silently directed the patrol to settle down and wait. The latrine was nothing more than a simple slit trench located out of sight of the CP. The NVA officers evidently appreciated privacy when tending to nature's calls.

A half hour dragged by before one of the NVA officers came down the narrow trail. He carried an entrenching tool in one hand and some paper in the other. It looked like an old magazine that had been ripped apart.

As the Goons watched, he dropped his trousers and squatted down over the trench. He strained and crapped not knowing that Archie and Blue had each taken a side of the track and had moved up a short distance from him.

The man finished and wiped himself with the magazine pages. Dutifully he took the entrenching tool and tossed dirt on top of his feces. After rearranging his clothing, he began to go back rapidly the way he had come.

But the two Black Eagles hit him simultaneously.

Archie thrust a gag into the NVA's mouth and Loco bound his hands in a quick, efficient attack that left the officer on his feet. Disoriented and surprised, the man felt his Tokorev pistol being taken from his holster. Archie and Loco hustled him back toward the latrine and into the jungle.

The patrol moved rapidly and the prisoner had trouble keeping up. He was also having difficulty breathing with the gag in his mouth. The North Vietnamese's eyes were open wide and he snuffed through his nose in a rapid, agitated manner.

"This guy's gonna suffocate!" Blue said holding onto one arm.

Loco, grasping the other, shook his head. "That don't mean shit. We got to leave the gag in. If this bastard don't mind dying, he'll yell if we take it out."

Archie, at the head of the patrol, kept the pace up. He glanced back from time to time to make sure there was no trouble. But when he saw the prisoner collapse to the ground, he halted and hurried back. "What's going on?" He looked at their captive. "The guy's face is turning blue, Loco!"

"Get the gag out quick!" Loco said.

Blue bent down and pulled the cloth away. The NVA gasped and took deep breaths. Finally he settled down, then let out a horrendous yell:

"Curu toi voi!"

The gag went straight back in. Loco sat down on the prisoner as the rest of the patrol took up a circular defense pattern. After a full five minutes of waiting, Loco jerked the NVA to his feet.

"You want to keep going now?" Archie asked.

"Yeah," Loco said. "But keep the pace down so this guy don't have no more trouble."

"Gotcha," Archie said.

They passed the next four hours in slow but continuous movement. Luckily, they ran into no more problems. When they reached the edge of the swamp, everyone was so tired that Loco was forced to give them a break.

"We got at least two more hours of tough traveling through that stinking water," Loco said. "We got to take a rest or we'll never make it."

The men set up another impromptu perimeter. Loco and the prisoner occupied the center. The NVA officer's eyes were wide with fear and anger. He constantly looked around, trying desperately to spot some means of escape.

"Hey," Loco said to him with a heavy nudge to the shoulder. "We're taking you to the land of the big PX. So calm down, huh? Di cham loi! I don't want you to get excited."

The prisoner couldn't seem to understand. He looked at Loco with an expression that seemed to be a mixture of

73

loathing and hatred.

"Whew!" Loco said. "I hope I never meet you in a dark alley some night when I'm drunk. You'd do a job on me, I bet!"

The patrol rested a scant quarter of an hour, but it was enough for them to catch their breath and rid themselves of some of the burning fatigue that had been sapping their strength. Loco grabbed the prisoner and hauled him to his feet. He signaled to the others. "Okay, guys. Let's go."

Archie went to the point as the others took up their positions once more. The scout was once again in ankle deep water. He dreaded the thought of going back into the slime of the swamp. But at least it meant the Goons were closer to home.

Then he almost bumped into the NVA supply detail.

The Reds, lugging rations on litters, were as surprised as Archie. But the Black Eagle reacted quicker. He raised the muzzle of his M16 and pumped the trigger, sweeping the NVA with rapid but inaccurate fire.

One toppled to the ground while his buddies dropped their burden and returned fire with their AK47s. Loco, quickly sizing up the situation, knew he had to consolidate the patrol in order to fight through.

"Fall back, Archie!" he yelled. "Quickly! Blue! Move on for'd!"

The prisoner, taking advantage of the confusion and turmoil amidst the roaring fusillades, suddenly twisted loose from Loco's grasp. He ran toward the NVA supply detail, unable to shout with the gag in his mouth. Their reaction was normal for the circumstance. Every one of them blasted at him. The unfortunate man's progress was halted as he shuddered under the impact of dozens of bullets before crumpling to the ground.

Loco continued to command his men through the action. "As skirmishers! For'd! Fire at will!"

The Goons swept toward the enemy, their combined fire sweeping back and forth. The enemy supply detail, not really prepared, was mowed down in the bursts of 5.56 millimeter slugs.

Enemy firing suddenly sounded from the rear.

"Goddamn!" Blue shouted. "More of 'em on the way! Them guys react quick!"

Trang Ngo, the ARVN ranger, turned and knelt down. He squeezed off two rounds and as many NVA stumbled to the ground while the rest of the patrol pulled back into the swamp. Ngo jumped up and ran to join them.

Loco and Ky Luyen provided covering fire while he rushed through a hail of enemy fire. In the meantime, Blue and Archie had taken cover behind a mang-cau-dai tree. They hosed full automatic streams of fire into the attacking enemy as Loco, Ngo, and Ky scampered toward them.

The patrol reassembled and set up a base of fire. Each man swept his muzzle back and forth, overlapping the guys on his side. The enemy, a rifle section, took immediate heavy casualties as they made another assault. They wisely pulled back, unable to make an effective attack into the swamp.

"Okay, boys," Loco said. "Now we run straight into that fucking swamp. And we go as fast as we can."

They sloshed through the water as the sounds of more arriving NVA could be heard out in the jungle. But it was impossible for the Reds to pursue the Goons.

Finally the patrol hit waist-deep water. Archie laughed. "I never thought I'd say it, but I love this ol' swamp!"

Chapter 8

Archie signaled back toward the patrol to drop to cover. As the other Goons ducked into the concealment of the thick jungle brush, Archie—his M16 at the ready—eased forward to the edge of a jackfruit tree. He peered around it and recognized a rather peculiar looking stand of jungle plants that surrounded a bent palm. It was always his habit to take note of various unusual features in the natural terrain where he operated. In the boondocks and its dearth of signposts, this was the only way to keep oneself oriented.

Now, recognizing the unusual vegetation and sure of his position, he took a deep breath and crawled around the tree. From that point on, he traveled straight ahead, exercising great caution. He knew he was close to friendly lines, but there was still the danger of some trigger-happy or nervous individual taking a shot at him.

"Calcitra!" someone said from out in front of the scout.

Archie quickly responded to the challenge with the proper password: "Clunis!"

"C'mon in, Archie," came Malpractice McCorckel's voice. "We're covering you."

After motioning the patrol to follow him, Archie led them across the front lines and back into friendly territory. He squatted down beside Malpractice as the rest of the Goons made their individual appearances.

"How's it been going?" Archie asked.

"Pretty quiet," Malpractice answered. "There ain't even been any enemy scouting activity. But we heard a firefight off in the distance. Was that you guys?"

"Sure was," Archie answered.

Malpractice counted each individual as the patrol came through the lines. "I see you didn't get a prisoner."

"It's a long story," Archie remarked. "I'll fill you in later."

He followed Loco and the others as they made their way back to Falconi's command post. They found the colonel anxiously awaiting them. The Goons, glad for the chance to finally relax, dumped their patrol harnesses and sat down while their team leader made his report. The smokers fished for their precious cigarettes, pulling out the sweat-soaked, crumpled packages to light up for the first time since leaving friendly territory.

Loco slowly shook his head. "Bad news. We lost our pris'ner, sir. He was a staff officer, too. We snatched the bastard back at their CP."

"Did you mark the headquarters on the map?" Falconi asked.

"Yes, sir," Loco said. "But it won't do us no good. From the looks of the thing, it's moved ever' two or three days anyhow."

"I'm not surprised," Falconi said. "Anyhow, tell me how you lost the prisoner."

"Well, sir, we stumbled across a supply detail and had a shoot out. The sonofabitch got hisself loose and ran straight at his buddies."

Falconi nodded knowingly. "And they shot him to pieces."

"They ruined his whole day, sir," Loco said. "But we got a hell of a map for you." He turned the marked document over to the Black Eagle commander.

Falconi studied the markings. Loco had used the proper map symbols, so the colonel could tell the locations of heavy machine guns, mortars, and recoilless rifles without having to ask what was at each location. Even the types of supplies at each dump was easy to see.

"There's that CP, sir," Loco said pointing. "But like I said, it prob'ly ain't there anymore."

"Especially since a prisoner was captured at that particular spot," Falconi added. "But that was a damned good job, Loco. Well done."

"I'm real sorry about losing that POW, sir," Loco said. "It was my fault. I had him in my hands, but when the shooting started, I lost my concentration. He jerked away from me."

"It's all right," Falconi said. "You and the Goons did a damn good day's work."

"Thank you, sir," Loco said. "At least we got some good targets for them F4 Phantoms."

Colonel Long Kuyen sitting nearby chuckled. "Are you going to give him the news, or me?"

"What news?" Loco inquired.

"It's good news and bad news," Falconi said.

"Oh, shit!" Loco exclaimed. "Tell me the good news first."

"The good news is that we've got air support laid on," Falconi said.

"What's the bad news?"

"We won't be getting any jet fighter support," Falconi said.

"It don't matter, sir," Loco said. "In a place like this, we can use some o' them South Vietnamese Air Force T-28s to advantage, can't we?"

"We don't even have that," Falconi remarked.

Loco frowned. "Then just what the fuck do we have, sir?"

"You know Donegan, Choy, and—"

"McKeever!" Archie Dobbs interrupted. "Sir! That's good news, bad news, and worst news!"

Blue Richards rolled his eyes. "Do you mean we're gonna have an old PBY as our support aircraft?"

"Our *only* support aircraft?" Loco added.

"That's it," Falconi said. "Don't worry. They did a good job for us when we fought that NVA tank outfit in Laos, didn't they?"

"Sir, they blew up one of *our* tanks," Archie reminded him.

"It was an accident," Falconi pointed out.

"I hope they don't have no more of them mishaps," Blue said.

"Are you kidding?" Archie sneered. "Them stout-swilling bastards ain't drawed a sober breath since I knowed 'em. Donegan would fly straight into a mountain if he saw some obscure advantage to it. That goddamned Choy is a complete whacked-out Chinese guy that thinks he's Irish, and that shit-for-brains McKeever is as dumb as a post."

"Okay," Falconi said. "Before this goes too far, just let me say a couple of things about that crew. Donegan would most certainly *not* fly into a mountain. But he'd damned well risk doing it to get a mission done."

Archie felt a little chastised. "Yes, sir."

"And Choy may have adopted Irish ways but he's as good at navigating in the sky as you are on the ground, Archie," Falconi pointed out. "He's a hell of a guy. He could be living in luxury in Taiwan, but he's got the balls to go after the adventurous life."

Archie, proud of his own reputation as a land navigator and tracker, shrugged. "Okay, Colonel. He's damn good."

"Donegan is drawing a full naval pension after twenty-six years of service," Falconi said. "Hell! He could be sitting in his rocker back in San Diego and enjoying the good life, but he's out here flying missions for Air America."

"Yes, sir," Archie said.

"And McKeever—" Falconi hesitated.

Now Archie grinned. "Yes, sir?"

"Well—he's good with engines and—"

"Go on, sir."

Falconi chuckled. "Okay. He's as dumb as a post. You win that one."

By then the deep, dark tropical night had settled in over the jungle. "Any more special jobs for us, sir?" Loco asked.

Falconi shook his head. "Get some sleep. Tomorrow is a big day."

"What's on tomorrow?"

"We're hitting the NVA again," Falconi said. "I'll radio the map coordinates of your recon back so Choy will know where to have McKeever drop the bombs. This will also help Calvin and his mortar boys lay out a barrage."

"Then?" Archie asked.

"Then we go in and see if we can kick their butts," Falconi said.

"C'mon, guys," Loco said. "I got an idea that we won't be getting any more chances to sleep for awhile."

"Either that or we'll get that long, permanent nap," Archie said.

The Goons followed Loco Padilla back to their team bivouac area. Everyone settled in for a good night's sleep, while up on the MLR the troops went into their night security routine.

While Operation Bo-Binh went into a lull out in the jungle, a bit of activity continued back in Hai-Cat. And it had nothing to do with partying at the beach. Choy was hard at work on his map, working out a course to fly from the coordinates that Falconi had radioed back to the CIA headquarters.

Out at the aircraft, McKeever was working his burly butt off getting the PBY ready for the next day's deadly duties. The tropical night was hot, but the big ex-sailor worked in serene calm as he tended to the many chores he had to complete. He spoke soothingly to the engines as he wiped oil off the spark plugs. This was his final activity after checking out the fuel pressure transmitter balance vents.

When he finished, McKeever stood up and gave the big flying machine a loving look. "You is tuned as tight as a virgin's puss," he said. "Now ain't that nice?"

Back in Fagin's office, Donegan was huddled in conference with Fagin and Andrea Thuy. They, too, were going along on the air support mission to act as side gunners on the heavy Browning .50 caliber machine guns mounted in the waist section of the aircraft.

The intrepid air crew finally knocked off work at a bit past midnight. Each turned in to get what sleep they could before dawn. Donegan and Choy were a bit nervous. Each downed some extra Guinness Stouts to help them drift off to sleep. Both Chuck Fagin and Andrea Thuy were unable to fall asleep. The two administrators lay wide-eyed and alert in their respective bungalows, waiting impatiently for the night to pass.

But Mike McKeever had put the entire assignment out of his mind. He relaxed for a while, looking at the pictures in a couple of comic books. That is how he always perused the colorful publications. The mechanic never bothered to try to read any of the words in the speech balloons above the characters' heads. It was a bit too much for him. So he enjoyed the artwork and drank down his own Guinnesses, completely at peace with the world.

After the long night finally drifted by and the sun began to rise above the far horizon on the South China Sea, the group stirred back to life. They followed the usual morning routine, but this time there was a bit of hurry to it. Following hasty showers, they dressed and downed quick, scanty breakfasts. Within three-quarters of an hour of rising, the entire bunch were seated inside the PBY, ready to go to war.

The engines warmed up under Donegan's expert touch, while Choy, seated at the navigator's station, rechecked the coordinates sent in by Falconi. When he was satisfied that the previous night's work had been accurate, he went up and took the copilot's seat beside Donegan.

The pilot gunned the engines and headed out into the lagoon for takeoff. "Can you find them places?"

"Piece of cake!" Choy happily answered.

McKeever, Fagin, and Andrea stood behind them as the PBY moved across the water. McKeever reported, "The machine guns is loaded. The bombs is in the racks. We be ready."

"What about fuel?" Donegan asked with a wink at Choy. He liked to kid McKeever, who never caught on to the ribbing.

McKeever frowned. "What does 'em say yer fuel gauges?"

"They indicated they are full," Donegan said.

"Then don't be worried on 'em," McKeever said. "Fly this bird."

"Okay," Donegan. "Just kidding, McKeever."

"Har! Har!" McKeever said, sneering.

"Let's check assignments once more before takeoff," Donegan said. "Choy will be the bombardier and man the front gun."

"Right!" Choy called out.

"Fagin will take the right side gun, and Andrea the left side gun."

"Right!" they acknowledged.

"And McKeever will take the tunnel gun," Donegan said.

"Huh?"

"I said that you'll take the tunnel gun," Donegan repeated.

"I know that. You already told me," McKeever said. "Cheez!"

Now the aircraft picked up speed, sticking to the smooth water of the lagoon. As soon as it reached the rougher waves on the far side of the breakwater, the suction on the hull broke and the old PBY was airborne and rapidly climbing.

"Course!" Donegan sang out.

"Three-four-four!" Choy answered. "I go to bombardier's position now. I give you changes when it is time."

They flew on for an hour with Choy making a couple of corrections when he saw the necessity of the action. Finally the Chinese navigator announced, "Okay, Donegan. Now is time to call Falconi."

Donegan hit the transmit switch and spoke into the microphone. "Checkmate, this is Aircraft. Over."

Falconi's voice came back loud and clear. "Aircraft, this is Checkmate. You're right on time for that first bombing run if you're ready. Over."

"Damn right we're ready, Checkmate. Put your hands over your ears. We're coming in like a Saturday night whore—hot and cheap!"

Choy, calculating at lightning speed, was now in command as the bombardier. The aircraft was completely under his control and it was up to Donegan to fly per his instructions. Choy checked the altimeter at his station. "Drop to two thousand feet—hold steady . . . steady . . . three degree right . . . steady . . . two degree right . . . quick . . . steady . . . hold steady . . ." He now closed his eyes and counted off seconds to himself. When he reached ten he hit the bomb release that opened the racks on the wing. "Bombs away! Turn! Turn!"

Donegan, his teeth clenched tight, pushed forward on the throttle as he made a climbing turn.

Down on the ground the entire ranger battalion was tensed. Although they could hear the PBY, they could barely catch glimpses of it as the aircraft roared past them above the tree canopy overhead.

Suddenly the sounds of detonating bombs racked the jungle.

The Black Eagles and ARVN troops could feel the concussion and the ground shaking. Everyone instinctively

83

cheered out of elation and excess nervous energy.

Falconi spoke into his microphone, "Forward all commandos. To the attack!"

The leading assault echelon was Sergeant Major Top Gordon's Second Commando. The senior noncommissioned officer and his men surged forward out of the fighting positions and moved rapidly forward toward the enemy MLR. They made contact within moments and a fierce firefight broke out up and down the line.

The combined blasting of M16s and AK47s was deafening in the confinement of the jungle. It grew in intensity until the superior defensive location of the North Vietnamese began to tell against Top's more exposed men. The attack lost its momentum as casualties began to mount. Then, in spite of heroic efforts, the commando's progress ground to a halt.

"Checkmate," Top radioed to Falconi. "They brought us to a standstill. My boys can't go no further under these circumstances. Over."

"Roger," Falconi said. "I'll bring in a strafing run. Pull back fifty meters."

Now it was Donegan's voice breaking in. "I monitored that transmission, Checkmate. We're coming in with all guns blazing. Get your fucking heads down! Now! Out."

Choy, with his bombardier's chores done, manned his machine gun in the nose turret. "Gunners, ready!" he yelled in the intercom.

Fagin, Andrea, and McKeever tensed at their own weapons. Each one nervously pulled back an extra time on the charging handle.

Donegan, following Choy's directions, came in at treetop level, concentrating on two things—flying level and maintaining the correct course.

"Okay!" Choy yelled. "Fire! Fire!"

All four heavy machine guns chugged rapidly, making Donegan's job that much harder. The recoil of the weapons tugged and pushed at the PBY, making it shudder through the air. But it didn't affect the accuracy of the sprays of big .50-caliber bullets. The gunners hosed the jungle with wide sweeps of the guns. McKeever, in the tunnel and firing backward, did a sort of follow-up as they swooped across the battlefield.

"Okay! Break!" Choy hollered.

Donegan, sweating heavily with the effort, took them into another steep, climbing turn.

Falconi listened as the PBY turned away. He got back on the radio. "Checkmate Two," he transmitted to Top Gordon. "Resume your attack. Out."

Once more the Second Commando attacked. This time the enemy defensive effort was much weaker. Top's combat unit hit a couple of tough, stubborn pockets of resistance where some dedicated NVA had decided to make a last stand, but these were neutralized with a combination of firepower and grenades at close quarter. Top and his men swept on past them.

The heavy machine guns had done a lot of damage. Bodies lay scattered around, and it looked as if the North Vietnamese positions had been hastily abandoned. Enemy equipment was scattered around, and a few wounded moaned piteously for mercy.

The attack picked up speed and Top reported his progress.

Falconi then ordered the First and Third commandos forward. The entire battalion moved straight ahead into enemy fire. The Black Eagle commander, along with Colonel Long Kuyen, formed up as skirmishers with the Goons.

With M16s at the ready, they advanced into a hell of what could only turn out to be one of the fiercest firefights of the whole damned Vietnam War.

Chapter 9

Major Tanh Hyun, commander of the North Vietnamese infantry battalion, cursed Russian workmanship as his R-108 radio crackled with static. He had heard the approach of the aircraft with great surprise. The officer had been even more shocked at the sound of a rapid series of high explosives that could only be aerial bombs. His attempts to make contact with his forward units to obtain a situation report had been futile.

"We will not be in the dark long," said his second-in-command, Captain Cuong Ngoi. "It is the battalion procedure to use runners and messengers when radio communication fails."

"I know the procedures, Comrade Captain!" Hyun snapped. The lack of accurate and up-to-date information was making him very irritable. His position, far to the south of normal NVA operations, was precarious enough without unreliable communication equipment making things more difficult. "I wrote the operating procedures we are following. Do you not remember?"

"Toi tec," Ngoi apologized.

"And these cursed radios are always failing, are they not?"

Captain Ngoi swallowed nervously. "I was merely pointing out—"

He was interrupted by small-arms fire erupting toward

the front lines. After building up to a roaring crescendo, it faded somewhat.

Hyun was about to settle down to wait for a runner to appear when once more he heard the airplane. This time, heavy machine gun fire could be detected within the roar of its engines. Now, out of control and livid with rage, he grabbed the microphone of the radio and screamed into it, "Chuyen gi vay? Answer me!"

Once more fighting could be heard. The sound was that of tremendous salvos that roared continually. Whatever was going on up on the MLR was being punctuated with the blasts of a fierce battle.

Hyun yelled again. "Chuten gi vay?"

When he finally received an answer, the speaker on the Russian radio crackled intermittently with the sound of an excited commo man's voice. "We—" Crackle! "—attacked by—"

Crackle! "—withdraw!"

"Do *not* pull back," Hyun transmitted back. "Durng dung-day! Hold your positions!"

Then the radio went dead.

Hyun tossed the microphone down in disgust. "Until the runners show up—if they do—we will be in the dark."

"Yes, Comrade Major," Captain Ngoi said. He knew the black rages that could sweep over his commander and he did not wish to witness such emotional fury. Hyun's face would turn purple, and in the end some hapless lower ranking unit leader would be taken out and summarily shot. Ngoi was glad he held no commands at that particular time.

When word finally managed to reach them from the front, not one but two messengers made appearances at the battalion command post. The first uttered a quick report, the words of his company commander quickly but carefully memorized:

"Comrade Major," he said breathlessly. "Our left flank is exposed. The enemy has attacked persistently and fiercely. The First Company has pulled back to reserve defensive position and is holding."

Hyun quickly switched his gaze to the second runner. "Co? What is your message, Comrade Soldier?"

The man, wounded in the arm, was pale from loss of blood. He gasped and swayed a bit, fighting to control himself before he could speak. "Comrade Major," he wheezed. "The Second Company is overrun. We have broken contact and pulled back."

"I see," Hyun said fighting to retain control over his emotions. He did not like common soldiers to see him in an excited mood. The major always thought it best that the men under his command consider him cool and calm under all circumstances—good or bad. He spoke in a quiet voice. "Were you bombed?"

"Yes, Comrade Major," the soldier said. He pointed to the field bandage on his arm. "I was hit by shrapnel. The bombs blew a big hole in our front line. Many men were killed. Then the enemy riflemen attacked. We fought hard, but we were too stunned."

"Thank you, Comrade Soldier," Hyun said. "Go to the aid station and have them check your arm. Then it's back to your company."

"Yes, Comrade Major."

Hyun dismissed the other messenger with a wave of his hand. Then he grabbed Ngoi's sleeve. "Tell the mortar section leader to fire three rounds of high explosive from each weapon. Have the shells drop on the front lines."

"But, Comrade Major," Ngoi protested. "Perhaps the Second Company has retaken that portion of our positions."

"Then they will die for the greater glory of the Vietnamese people!" Hyun bellowed. "Obey me now!"

Ngoi saluted fearfully, then rushed off to obey the order.

Falconi trotted forward with the Goons spread out on

both sides of him. Colonel Kuyen, bringing up the rear, stuck close to the ARVN radio operator, who labored along with the AN/PRC-77 radio on his back.

Directly to their front, the weapons squad of Second Commando moved as fast as possible under their load of machine guns. Threading their way through the enemy dead and the remnants of the NVA fighting positions, they followed the rifle squads ready to give them fire support when needed.

The group had made twenty-five meters when the first mortar rounds hit.

The explosions erupted in rapid blasts of orange flame and black smoke. The detonations were deafening, sending out waves of concussions that buffeted the eardrums of Falconi and his men. Several of the ARVN rangers were bleeding from the ears, but they took no notice of the condition as the world around them turned into a thundering, roaring hell. Flying shrapnel in the area struck each other and made sparks as they zipped through the air in lightning-quick swarms of metal fragments. The shards slapped men into bloody hunks that blew them apart in a horrible combination of red spray and charred flesh.

Falconi knew that there was no point in pulling back. The only thing that awaited them rearward was more death and destruction. They had to charge through it.

"Move on! Move on!" he ordered. "The man that *stays* here, *dies* here!"

Leaving the dead and dying behind, they picked up their pace and ran toward the front. The group kept going for another twenty-five meters until Top Gordon and Steve Matsuno appeared with the remnants of the Second Commando.

Top was streaked with a combination of sweat and battle smoke. His face was so dirty that the whiteness of his teeth, even though he clenched a half-smoked stogie between them, was dazzling in the jungle gloom. "My attack is broke up, sir," he reported. "We can't move no more. I'm getting tired o' this shit." He didn't speak in a complaining voice. Rather it was the tone of a man anxious to turn things around to his own advantage.

"Hang tight," Falconi told him. The colonel understood perfectly how the sergeant major felt. The Black Eagle commander grabbed the handset from his radio man and issued terse orders through the instrument. "All Checkmates, this is Checkmate," he said. "Everyone pull back fifty meters and realign the attack formation. Do it now. Out." Then he issued another transmission. "Aircraft, this is Checkmate. We need more help from you. Over."

Up in the aircraft, which was circling five kilometers away, Donegan quickly answered. "We got no bombs left, Checkmate. But we can make another strafing run. Over."

"Go for it!" Falconi broadcasted.

"Roger," Donegan said. He turned on the intercom and spoke to his crew. "We got another strafing mission, folks. Let's get to them guns." He banked the aircraft and headed down for treetop level. Pulling up at the right altitude, he pulled back on the throttle and began the run.

Choy gave the word when they were at the correct location. "Okay! Fire! Fire!"

Donegan fought the controls against the recoil as the four heavy machine guns shook the hell out of the PBY. He watched the artificial horizon on his attitude indicator instrument jumping crazily while he did his best to keep the wings as level as possible.

Suddenly the aircraft shuddered violently and lost altitude. "We're hit!" Donegan yelled instinctively. He pulled back on the wheel and finally got the PBY back under control, but not before it clipped the tops of several tall trees.

Fagin leaned forward to glance out the side blister. "Shit!" he said to himself. He turned on his intercom.

"Donegan, the starboard engine is smoking."

"Roger," Donegan said. "McKeever, take a look."

"Okay," came back the mechanic's ponderous voice. A couple of beats later, he said, "It's gonna flame up."

Donegan immediately feathered the engine, then hit the automatic fire extinguisher. "Ever'body hang on!" he yelled, starting a violent turn. "We're getting the hell outta here!"

McKeever made another report. "The port stabilizer is aloose, Donegan. How does she handle?"

"Mushy as shit," Donegan replied. He applied extra pressure on the starboard rudder to correct the wild yawing of the PBY. "Goddamn it! This baby is going down!"

McKeever angrily yelled back, "No! It ain't gonna crash. I tuck too much good care of it. You fly this bird, Donegan. You fly her or I'm gonna slap you right up the side of your damn head. You bet I will!"

Fagin had trouble maintaining his balance as he hung on to the handles of his machine gun. "I say we get up to jump altitude and parachute outta here."

"Go ahead," McKeever said upset. "All you assholes jump. I'll stay here and fly her back to Hai-Cat. I be seeing you on the beach when you get back." He leered at them. "*If* you get back. There be a whole shitpot full of 'em NVA down there just awaitin' for you. Har! Har!"

By then Choy had crawled out of the bombardier's compartment and joined Donegan in the cockpit. He did some quick calculations. "Fly course one-seven-six."

"Roger," Donegan said fighting to turn the shaking aircraft.

Fagin's nervousness increased. "This motherfucker is gonna crash!"

"Hey!" McKeever bellowed. "You don't call my plane a motherfucker or I'll whop you one."

Finally Andrea's voice came over the intercom. It was calm and feminine, with a hint of motherliness in it.

"You great big men stop yelling. Do you hear me?"

Everyone settled down.

Andrea continued. "Now, Donegan. You fly us home."

"Yes, ma'am," Donegan replied.

"And Fagin," Andrea said. "Watch what you call this wonderful airplane."

"Okay," Fagin answered in a soft voice.

"And McKeever," Andrea instructed. "Don't talk bad to Fagin."

"Fuck him!"

"McKeever!" Andrea scolded.

"Yes, mum."

Choy interrupted. "What I do, Miss Andrea?"

"Show Tim which direction to fly," she answered.

"Yes, Miss Andrea."

As the aircraft continued on its way back to Hai-Cat, Ray Swift Elk made a check of his impromptu front line. He had reported sighting the PBY turning away from the battle site with one engine smoking.

Falconi took the news philosophically. He'd never known things to go right in combat yet. He had just managed to straighten the new MLR when the North Vietnamese made their counterattack. It was a bold move on their part.

Top's Second Commando, as usual, caught the brunt of the assault. He and his men dug in their heels and slugged back with a combination of M16 and machine gun fire. They only held up the NVA for a few brief moments before the Reds rolled straight into their positions.

Falconi knew the situation without being told. He radioed quick and terse instructions to the harried sergeant major. "Checkmate Two, pull back. Don't lose any more men if you can help it. We'll cover your flanks. Over."

Top's voice was strained as he answered. "Wilco, Checkmate. We'll pull back now. Out."

"Checkmates One and Three, cover Checkmate Two's flanks," Falconi said transmitting more instructions. He tossed the handset over to his radioman. "Hey, Goons!" he yelled.

Loco and his team gave the detachment commander their full attention.

"They need help up forward," Falconi said. "Go for it."

"Let's go, guys!" Loco said.

The team went less than twenty meters and found themselves up to their necks in the fighting. An advance squad of NVA infantry almost ran straight into them.

Blue and Ngo immediately hit the dirt and put out covering fire. Loco, Archie, and Ky maneuvered around through the jungle brush until they reached some cover offered by a grove of rattan. They wasted no time in pouring withering volleys of M16 fire into the enemy squad. The entire group of Reds crumpled under the salvos, but another squad quickly showed up to take their place.

Now Blue and Ngo had to hotfoot it back with the attackers on their heels. They dove into the rattan and turned to deliver more fire. Suddenly a cut-off group of ARVN rangers came in from the flank. Ngo sighted them and yelled. The South Vietnamese soldiers turned and raced through the fire toward the Goons.

"Tell 'em to get down!" Loco ordered.

Ngo shouted, "Nam xuong!"

Now the Goons increased their fire into the enemy and broke up their formation, but, as before, more appeared.

"Okay, Ngo," Loco said. "Tell your pals to run like hell."

"Tien len!" Ngo hollered. "Mau len!"

The rangers raced back and passed the rattan grove as they headed to rejoin their unit. The Goons leaped and

93

ran after them, every man congratulating himself for helping to pull off a damned good cover-and-run operation.

"Napoleon could'a used us at Waterloo!" Archie crowed.

"Fuck Napoleon!" Blue yelled back. "I'd rather help ol' Massa Lee out at Gettysburg."

"Just help old Falconi in Vietnam!" Loco growled at them.

They reached their commanding officer, who was still directing the fighting by radio. He was mad as hell. "This is the most frustrating goddamned operation we've ever been on!" he said to no one in particular. He grabbed the handset. "All Checkmates, pull back! Withdraw!" He spat. "Shit! Why don't I just say the right thing?" He spoke once again into the microphone. "Retreat, goddamn it! Haul ass! Bug out!"

Archie Dobbs and Blue Richards, veteran Black Eagles, stared at their commander incredulously. They had never seen him in such a state of mind.

"Damn!" Archie said. "This situation must have split wide open."

"You know something," Blue said. "For the first time since I been a Black Eagle, I really think we're headed down the tubes."

"Headed?" Loco said. "We're there, pal. We just ain't got enough sense to own up to the fact our asses is kicked!"

Chapter 10

Colonel Robert Falconi, United States Army, was normally not an excitable man.

But when he did get angry, there were subtle little signs that warned his men that their commanding officer was in no mood for any bullshit. It showed in the way he frowned a bit and kept his eyes opened wider than usual. His voice had an edge that also served as a signal of a potential storm of temper. That latter condition was evident even over the radio as he spoke into the microphone:

"All Checkmates, this is Checkmate. Send your deputy commanders to the Charlie Papa now. I say again and for the last time. Send your deputy commanders to the Charlie Papa *now!* Out."

Needless to say, Captain Ray Swift Elk, Sergeant Major Top Gordon, and Master Sergeant Malpractice Mc-Corckel wasted no time in dispatching messieurs Garcia, Matsuno, and Olson in a most quick and efficient manner to the Colonel Falconi's CP—the Charlie Papa—the command post. This had been set up after the Black Eagles and ARVN rangers had bugged out far enough to break contact with the North Vietnamese attackers.

When the three assistant leaders of the assault commandos arrived, they found the Goons had also been summoned. Loco Padilla's team stood respectfully assembled in Falconi's august presence.

The deputy commando leaders waited to see what the colonel wanted. Their commanding officer didn't take long in explaining:

"The enemy is pushing us around because of his heavy weaponry," he announced. "Calvin Culpepper has done his best with counter-battery fire, but there is no way he can match up the few mortars we have with that reinforced bunch the NVA have been using to break up our attacks."

"Are we gonna get some more mortars then, sir?" Gunnar Olson asked. He was particularly fond of heavy weapons. A former helicopter door gunner, he was sometimes referred to as "Gunner Gunnar" by the rest of the Black Eagles detachment.

Falconi shook his head. "Even if there are some available, they would never be able to get them to us in time to salvage the situation."

"What the hell?" queried Paulo Garcia. "Have we lost this frigging battle?"

"Yeah. We most assuredly have," Falconi said. "But we haven't lost the campaign yet. But I'm afraid it's an undeniable fact we're so close to total defeat that I'm beginning to get a Custer complex."

"Then what are we gonna do, sir?" asked Steve Matsuno. He quickly added, "If you don't mind me asking."

Falconi smiled sardonically. "We could call it quits, I guess. As a matter of fact, the SITREP I just composed and sent back to the rear would be enough to warrant a rapid abandonment of this area of operation."

"Are we really that bad off, sir?" Archie asked.

"Archie, my boy," Falconi said in a fatherly tone, "there is not a staff officer alive in any army of the world today who would not quickly advise us to abandon this campaign and withdraw completely." The colonel smiled and shrugged.

The Black Eagles didn't smile back at their commander. Archie Dobbs almost sneered. "There ain't been nobody that kicked our asses yet, sir."

"Then by God, we better do something damned quick to salvage this situation," Falconi said.

"We're with you, sir," Loco said.

Paulo Garcia was more direct. "Is it correct to assume that you've reached some sort of conclusion, sir?"

"I may have come up with a solution," Falconi said. "But let me warn you. It's risky as hell and has as much chance of getting us killed as making us come out winners."

"What are we going to do, sir?" Archie Dobbs asked. He almost dreaded finding out what the answer to the question would be.

"We are going to make a parachute assault on the rear of the NVA positions and take out those goddamned heavy mortars of theirs," Falconi said. "This operation will include Corporal Trang Ngo of the ARVN rangers. He has proven a brave and valuable teammate. Colonel Kuyen has graciously allowed him to go along on this operation."

Ngo beamed with pride at the compliment. He'd grown close to the others in the Goon Team through mutual respect and friendship.

Falconi continued. "I've been in contact with Hai-Cat through the ranger battalion's commo center and I've learned that the PBY was damaged rather extensively during that last strafing run they made for us. But McKeever is working overtime and has that problem well in hand. Fagin assures me the aircraft will be ready by the time we get back there."

"Are we going all the way back to Hai-Cat, sir?" Archie asked.

"Yes," Falconi answered. "But only long enough to draw chutes and fly right back to this great big fuck-up we're involved in here."

"You mean straight back into this battle you say we've lost?" Blue Richards asked.

97

"Exactly," Falconi said.

"Okay, sir," Blue said.

Loco Padilla was more interested in the technical aspects of the plan. "Are we going to jump the PBY, Colonel?" the marine sergeant asked. "I didn't think that baby was rigged proper for personnel exits."

"They have a trap door arrangement as is used on C-119s when monorail equipment drops are made," Falconi said. "We'll go through there. The opening is small, but we won't be carrying much gear."

"We're human cargo, are we?" Steve Matsuno asked with a wry grin.

"Exactly," Falconi said. "Now here's our organization. I'll head the thing up, naturally, and you'll be divided into two fire teams. Loco will take Fire Team Alpha with Archie, Blue, and Ngo. Ngo will be the automatic rifleman and Blue will be the grenadier."

"What about M203s?" Blue asked referring to the grenade launchers that could be attached to M16s.

"We will draw them with the chutes," Falconi said. "Fagin already has them in his hot little hands for us. Now Fire Team Bravo is going to be led by Paulo. Steve Matsuno, Gunnar, and Ky will be with him. Steve will keep his M16 on full auto while Gunnar acts as grenadier."

Gunnar was happy with the assignment. He liked firing the 40-millimeter grenades.

"And here's exactly how we do it," Falconi said. "It's sweet and simple—and deadly. We'll make a low-altitude drop at eight hundred feet onto the flat, open area the Goons found on their patrol. According to the map it is less than three hundred meters from the mortar battery."

"What is the rest of our guys and the ARVN ranger battalion gonna be doing, sir?" Archie asked.

"At the exact time we exit the aircraft, they will launch an all-out assault," Falconi explained. "When the mortar battery is neutralized, they should be able to press on and wrap up this Operation Bo-Binh quite handily."

"What if things turn real mean and shitty and we don't take out the mortars?" Paulo Garcia asked.

"Then the attack will fail and those of us caught behind the enemy lines will either end up dead or as POWs," Falconi said flatly.

"Hell of a choice," Archie complained.

Gunnar Olson had a brighter attitude. "Well! I for one find the situation a real motivator for succeeding."

"Gunnar, you are too fucking much," Archie said under his breath.

"Okay, boys," Falconi said. "Let's get our gear and move out. Colonel Kuyen has vehicles waiting for us. We can be back in Hai-Cat in a couple of hours."

Early in the morning of the day following Falconi's decision to make an airborne assault, Mike McKeever made a final check on the cable splice. Finally satisfied, he crawled down from the tunnel gunner's compartment. "Awright, Donegan. Pull it forward the wheel," he said in his strange manner of speaking.

Up in the pilot's station, Tim Donegan eased the control column forward.

"Now move it back the wheel," McKeever hollered. He watched the elevator respond. "Okay, it be fixed." He joined the pilot at the navigator's table behind the cockpit, where Choy waited for them. "And that engine really hums now."

"Yeah," Donegan said. They'd finished checking out the damaged starboard engine barely an hour before. "Are you sure we ain't gonna have any problems with it?"

"The only thing was busted oil lines," McKeever said. "That's why she flared up. It's good the way you turned on the fire putter-outter so quick."

Choy, who had been working on his map, now stood up. "Okay. I got course down to gnat's ass. We ready."

The three climbed out the overhead hatch and stood up on the top of the fuselage. Below them, on the dock, eight Black Eagles and the ARVN ranger corporal who had arrived the previous evening had already donned their T-10 parachutes.

Chuck Fagin and Andrea Thuy were there too, watching as Falconi gave his men a final rigger check.

"I don't know why you bother wearing them reserve chutes," Donegan said to them. "At eight hunnerd feet you ain't gonna have time to pull 'em if the main fails."

"Oh, yeah?" Archie Dobbs called up. "If I get a malfunction, you just watch me!"

Donegan laughed. "Okay, sport. You're like the guy that got caught with another man's wife when the husband came home. When he asked where the back door was, she said there wasn't one."

"I know the story," said Archie. "Then he asked her where she wanted one, right?"

"Right," Donegan said. He looked at Colonel Robert Falconi. "Well, according to the ace mechanic McKeever we're ready to go now anytime."

"Do you have us coming in on a good, accurate azimuth, Choy?" Blue Richards asked as he got a tap on the head from Falconi to indicate his chute was okay.

"You betcha! I drop you personal on assistant gunner of third mortar from right," Choy said.

They laughed at Choy's humor as Falconi completed his inspection of the parachutes and equipment. The colonel turned to Fagin and Andrea. "This is it. So long and we'll see you later."

"Listen, Falconi," Chuck said under his breath. "You got every right in the world to call off that operation. Things are really shitty out there."

Andrea's concern for her lover was in her eyes, though her voice was calm. "Nobody would blame you, Robert. The situation is unsalvagable."

"Maybe I'm too damned dumb to know that," Falconi said. "Or too damned dumb to give a shit. I really don't

100

know which it is."

"You're just too damned stubborn," Andrea said. "Goodby, Robert." She gave him a quick kiss on the cheek.

Fagin offered his hand. "Go for it, if you must."

"Sure," Falconi said. He turned to his men. "Okay, guys. Let's make station time. There's an NVA mortar battalion waiting for us."

They clambered aboard and seated themselves inside the confines of the narrow fuselage. McKeever had rigged an anchor line for the jumpers to hook on their static line snap fasteners. Although he had faith in the mechanic's ability, Falconi didn't take any chances. He reached up and grabbed it, putting his full weight on the cable as he bounced up and down.

It was solid as a rock.

The PBY rocked gently on the water as the engines fired up. Donegan, working with his usual efficiency, had the aircraft off the South China Sea and into the air within a short period of time. He made a wide, lazy turn, then settled the bird down for its flight back to the hell of Operation Bo-Binh.

The Black Eagles were not too comfortable in their parachutes and weapons, but they knew the ride would only be a short one. They were thankful for that. The heat brought on by the low altitude of their flight caused them to become soaked in perspiration within a few minutes of takeoff. Not all that sweat was from the temperature and humidity, however. They were about to pull off the sort of operation that many military experts thought was not only obsolete but had perhaps always been unworkable—a parachute assault behind enemy lines. Helicopters had proved much superior in those sorts of operations. Unfortunately, none was available on the short notice needed.

The Black Eagles' parachutes were T-10s. The effi-

101

ciently designed devices were described officially as:

Parachutes, troop type, static line operated, bag deployed, pack assemblies.

It had a parabolic canopy with a thirty-five-foot nominal diameter and a twenty-four and a half foot projected diameter at the skirt. Its deployment sequence began when the jumper, after exiting the aircraft, fell to the end of the fifteen-foot static line. At that time the pack closing tie broke and the deployment bag fell free from the pack tray. Suspension lines played out of their stowage loops, then the canopy itself came out of the deployment bag to blossom open and lower the parachutist to the ground with a minimum of oscillation.

But sometimes it malfunctioned.

The brainy boys cold-bloodedly classified malfunctions into two categories: partial and complete. Some partials were caused when the canopy did weird things like inversions, cigarette rolls, or when it suffered blown gores. In cases like that, the jumper had some support and could expect a bit of time to deploy his reserve parachute in a set sequence of steps to safely continue his descent to the ground.

A complete malfunction, however, meant that nothing was working. In that case the only thing to do was immediately pull the ripcord on the reserve and hope for the best. But as the parachute instructor cheerfully told the student jumper, "Don't worry, pal. It ain't the fall that kills you—it's that sudden stop!"

Because of the low altitude of the jump, Falconi and the Black Eagles in the PBY would stand absolutely no chance of activating their reserve parachutes in case of malfunctions. The very best they could hope for was that they would get enough support from a partial malfunction to hit the ground with only enough force to cause minor injury. In the worst-case scenario, the injured man would be behind enemy lines unable to fend for himself.

As for a complete malfunction, the jumper would simply hurtle down to that "sudden stop."

102

Choy made an appearance. "Okay! Five minutes out."

Falconi stood up and walked to the exit hatch in the deck. "Buckle down your helmets," he called out.

The Black Eagles quickly fastened the chin straps of their helmets.

Falconi yelled, "Get ready!"

The men leaned forward, holding out the snap fasteners of their static lines to show they were ready.

"Stand up!"

They stood up and grasped the anchor line.

"Hook up!"

Static lines fasteners were snapped to the anchor line.

"Check static lines!"

They made sure the fifteen-foot devices were not misrouted under equipment.

"Check equipment!"

The rest of their gear went through another inspection.

"Sound off for equipment check!"

"Eight okay!" Ky Luyen shouted.

"Seven okay!" acknowledged Trang Ngo.

Gunnar Olson hollered, "Six okay!"

"Five okay!" That was Blue Richards.

Steve Matsuno let out, "Four okay!"

Archie Dobbs bellowed, "Three okay!"

Paulo Garcia shouted, "Two okay!"

"One okay," Loco announced.

Falconi grinned at the eager men. "What are you?"

"Airborne!" they shouted in unison.

"How far?"

"All the fucking way!"

McKeever, on the intercom, told Donegan they were all ready for the jump. Then he hit the hydraulic pump to open the trap doors.

Falconi gave out the next command which was for himself. "Stand in the door!"

He stood directly over the hatch while the stick of Black Eagle parachutists pressed closely to him. The colonel could see the tops of the trees looking like they were only a dozen or so feet below him.

Now McKeever, listening to Choy's instructions on the intercom, raised his hand as a signal. Falconi, watching him intently, tensed. McKeever dropped his hand and the colonel went through the hatch.

Falling face down, he felt the static line pulling out of the stowage loops, then the backpack as it broke loose. There was a swoosh as the big canopy whipped open above him. Falconi's legs swung under him and his feet went down. He instantly hit the ground hard, going into a proper parachute landing fall.

He hit the quick release box on the canopy and got up grasping his M16 rifle. The colonel watched as his men now began getting to their feet and moving toward him.

He checked his watch. They had but fifteen minutes to neutralize the NVA mortar battery.

Chapter 11

The Black Eagles left their abandoned parachutes spread out along the entire length of the drop zone. Neither time nor circumstances made it necessary—or even possible—to conceal the aerial devices. Within a very short time the NVA would most certainly be aware of the airborne infiltration. Also, the small attack force was pushed hard to meet their scheduled assault on the enemy mortar positions.

Tight-lipped and determined, the parachutists followed Colonel Falconi's orders as they moved off the flat, empty slice of Asian terrain. When they cleared the drop zone, the deadly and determined group formed up as skirmishers.

No one spoke a word as they approached the jungle's edge. Once inside the tree line, the attackers would have a scant fifteen meters before reaching the North Vietnamese mortar positions. Each man knew that split-second timing and being ready for the unexpected was all important. What they didn't know was that luck had worked against them. A recently posted enemy unit, acting as a reserve force, had moved into the same strip of rain forest to wait until they were needed. Worn out from a long period of constant combat, that particular group of NVA had established a bivouac between the Black Eagles and their objective.

The impending meeting of the two forces could not be described as congenial.

An alert Red perimeter guard sighted the infiltrators. For a brief second he was completely mystified by the unexpected sight of the enemy walking around in what was considered a safe rear area.

But he quickly recovered.

The sentry sounded the alarm, which resulted in sporadic small arms splattered outward from the NVA position.

Spurts of dust kicked up at the Black Eagles' feet and the angry zipping of 7.62-millimeter bullets zipped angrily around their heads as the enemy fusillades grew in momentum as more NVA came from their squad camp sites and joined the fighting on the bivouac perimeter.

Falconi didn't have time to ponder the unexpected situation. He had to get things moving fast. "Grenadiers!" the colonel yelled. "Up on line! Cover 'em, riflemen!"

Petty Officer Blue Richards and Sergeant Gunnar Olson raised the muzzles of their M203-equipped M16s and kicked loose M406 grenades. The projectiles arched up and fell directly into the midst of the NVA riflemen.

Now the rest of the parachute assault detachment began a combination of offensive and recon-by-fire shooting. While everyone else was on semiautomatic and pumping individual but closely spaced shots at the enemy, Trang Ngo and Steve Matsuno hosed 5.56-millimeter rounds from their weapons on full auto. They swept their muzzles back and forth to cover the front of their respective teams.

"Double-time!" Falconi commanded.

The group ran toward the woods, entered it, and leaped over the bodies of dead NVA who had gone down in the initial fighting. The Reds' buddies had wisely pulled back enough to find good cover. They poured back volleys of well-directed sprays of Kalashnikov slugs, which forced the Black Eagles to stop and return the fire.

Falconi didn't like the static condition one damned bit. He checked his watch and noted that the ARVN Ranger attack was due to start in less than five minutes.

"Grenadiers," he bellowed as he again called on the talents of his rifle grenade experts. "Move forward with M576 rounds. Everybody cover them."

Blue and Gunner loaded the multi-projectile canisters into the M203s and rushed toward the enemy at a crouch. The particular type of rounds they were about to fire could best be described as buckshot dispensing. The nasty little buggers were designed for close-in nasty fighting—which was exactly what they were engaged in at that explosive moment.

The M203 grenade launchers kicked and bucked as they dispensed their deadly loads. Leaves, branches, tree bark, and hunks of enemy soldiers flew into the air. Blue and Gunnar reloaded and cut loose twice more.

"Okay," Falconi said. "Go for broke!"

Now everybody was on their feet. They attacked with wild yells and rapid bursts of fire. The NVA who had survived the horrible maiming of the buckshot crumpled in undignified heaps, their last efforts at resistance futile. What had been an enemy rifle section was now nothing but broken bodies.

The Black Eagles raced through the bivouac area, leaping over cookfires that heated pots of rice destined to go uneaten. Falconi and his men hit the next stretch of rain forest that separated them from the enemy mortar battery.

Less than a dozen seconds later, they broke out of the jungle and into the battery's position. The enemy gunners, poised to fire the heavy weaponry, were caught flat-footed. A horrible swarm of slugs, buckshot, and shrapnel from other rifle grenades swept them off their feet, leaving the dead and dying around the mortar tubes.

It was that quick—and that final.

"Okay, guys," Falconi said. "We now own this hunk of real estate. We're going to have to hold it until the rest

107

of the battalion links up with us."

Wordlessly, grimly, and with a fierce determination, the Black Eagles formed a defensive perimeter around the rim of the battery area.

Archie Dobbs glanced at the human carnage scattered around the area. "Christ!" he exclaimed. "I hope we have better luck than those poor bastards!"

Captain Ray Swift Elk was in overall command of the battalion now that Colonel Falconi had gone on the parachute assault behind enemy lines. He had explicit orders to follow. These involved down-to-the-second timing similar to that of the infiltrators who now held the NVA mortar position.

As Colonel Long Kuyen waited beside him, the Sioux Indian studied the sweep hand on his watch, watching it move in what seemed to be slowness he found totally exasperating.

Ten . . . he licked his lips nervously . . . *nine* . . . *eight* . . . *seven* . . . the captain wiped at the sweat on his forehead . . . *six* . . . *five* . . . he held out his hand for the radio handset . . . *four* . . . *three* . . . Swift Elk placed it to his ear . . . *two* . . . he blew in the mouthpiece . . . *one* . . . the Sioux officer pushed the transmit button . . . *zero*—

"Attack! Attack! Attack!"

The rangers and their Black Eagle advisers surged forward as a living, yelling, cursing tide of blasting hell. All three commandos left their fighting holes and charged like besieged devils toward the enemy main line of resistance. Hitting hard, fast, and ruthlessly was the only way to enjoy any kind of initial success. Those facts had been relentlessly drilled into both the Black Eagles and the ARVN rangers.

Back in his own area, Chief Warrant Officer Calvin Culpepper was happy as hell to finally contribute his heavy weapon expertise to the cause.

108

"Fire mission! Shell HE! Fuse quick!" he commanded. The details of the barrage had been carefully worked out on his firing tables. "Charge four! Three rounds for effect! Fire!"

Each crew on the six mortars worked in unison. The gunners set the mortar rounds in the end of the tubes and dropped them to slide down to the firing pins. They repeated this twice more, sending a total of eighteen 81-millimeter shells lobbing up in a lazy trajectory that ended as they plunged in controlled dives into the NVA area.

Major Tanh Hyun, commander of the North Vietnamese battalion, had been facing the north listening to a fire fight that grew in intensity then suddenly died off. Without effective radio communications within his unit, he had no idea what was going on. But he rightly surmised the trouble was in the vicinity of his mortars. And that made the NVA officer nervous as hell. His entire plan of battle—both offensive and defensive—hinged on those mortars.

The major quickly dispatched Captain Cuong Ngoi to see firsthand what had occurred in an area that was supposed to be completely secure.

The captain had barely left when firing suddenly broke out in the south. As Major Hyun instinctively whirled in that direction, the second of numerous mortar explosions could be heard in the area of his MLR. The sound was different from the Chicom 82-millimeter shells his own troops had. That meant these particular rounds were unfriendly and were dropping in the midst of his command.

Hyun grabbed the Russian radio and tried to raise his front-line positions. Failing that, he grew enraged and kicked the useless instrument. Finally, so angry he could not contain himself, he jumped up and down on the communications gear, smashing it to bits.

At that moment Captain Cuong Ngoi returned from his errand. The sight of his furious commander did not make him feel any better about the news he had to deliver. "Comrade Major!" the captain fearfully reported. "The mortar battery is in enemy hands! And a reserve rifle section was wiped out."

"Co dung khong?" Hyun screamed, spittle splattering from his mouth.

Ngoi gulped and effected a weak smile. "I am sorry, Comrade Major. But it is true."

"How many of the running dogs of capitalism are there?" Hyun demanded to know.

"At least a dozen, Comrade Major," Ngoi answered quaking. "They appear to be American."

"What do you mean they *appear* to be?" Hyun demanded to know.

"There are Asians with them, but we cannot determine how many," Ngoi said.

Before the major could do any more insane bellowing, a young soldier acting as runner appeared. His face was streaked with sweat and he was panting so hard he could barely speak. "Comrade Major—a heavy attack—" he wheezed with great effort as he gained control over his voice. "Supported by mortar fire—all up and down—our line. We are hardpressed—the comrade company commanders respectfully—requests permission to—retreat—"

Now wanting to appear calm since an enlisted soldier was present, Hyun brought his emotions under control. "Thank you, Comrade Soldier. Return to the main line of resistance and tell all commanders they are ordered to hold at all costs. Tell all commanders they are ordered to hold *at all costs*. Ong hieu khong?"

"Yes, Comrade Major!"

"Tell them I will not tolerate withdrawal without further orders," Hyun said. "Our front lines must be held without fail. No sacrifice is too great." Then he scowled. "And tell them that anyone disobeying will be shot."

"Yes, Comrade Major!" He repeated the message to show he would repeat it faithfully. "We are to hold until further orders. Anyone who retreats will be shot."

"Duoc roi! Carry on, Comrade Soldier." Hyun turned to Ngoi. "Are there any other reserve units available?"

Ngoi, glad for a chance to be positive, enthusiastically nodded his head. "Yes, Comrade Major! There is an entire company only fifty meters from here. They are waiting to support any breakthroughs."

"We must get back those mortars!" Hyun hissed. "Order the reserve company to attack the enemy there. If there are only a dozen or so, the infiltrators will be outnumbered by twenty-to-one."

Ngoi saluted and rushed off to tend to the job.

The situation was hot and heavy up on the fighting front. The two forces—Black Eagle-led ranger commandos and NVA infantry—collided in the fighting that swirled through the blackened, blasted jungle.

Bitter hand-to-hand battles raged up and down the line as firefights took place at ranges less than five meters. Bayonets, knives, and even fists and boots were employed in the close quarters of eye-to-eye killing and maiming.

The air was thick with battle smoke and the hoarse, enraged bellowing of fighting men. In the midst of the roaring hell, the pathetic shrieks and cries of badly wounded men could also be heard.

The NVA line resisted stubbornly against the pressure from the rangers. For each instant that they gave a few grudging, bloody yards they would fight back, shooting and stabbing their way in a blood-soaked return to their original positions. This blasting hell-on-earth fighting left the dead and wounded of both sides lying side-by-side, death making comrades of them all.

Because of their own mulelike persistence, the rangers

finally forced a bulge in the NVA MLR. But Malpractice McCorckel and his Third Assault Commando were in deep shit.

"We're outnumbered here," he radioed back to Swift Elk. "We been seesawing back and forth across the front. Can you relieve some of the pressure? Over."

"Roger, Checkmate Three," the Sioux officer replied. He called up Calvin. "Give us another barrage of six rounds per tube. And raise it fifty meters. Over."

"Goddamn, sir!" Calvin yelled back in his radio. "The lines are too fluid! You could fight your way straight into our own mortar fire!"

"Damn your eyes, Buffalo Soldier!" Swift Elk yelled back. "Cut loose! Out!"

"Wilco," Calvin replied tersely.

In less than twenty seconds the first of thirty-six detonations erupted along the front line. The heavy shells slammed down from their trajectories, streaking to the ground and exploding upon impact, throwing out waves of concussion and spitting showers of white-hot hunks of steel.

The NVA infantrymen caught in the fire-and-metal storm melted under the onslaught. In that sector of the line, the Red forces disappeared.

At the same time the mortar barrage was blasting the hell out of the FEBA—the Forward Edge of the Battle Area—Ray Swift Elk raised Sergeant Major Top Gordon on the radio.

"This is Checkmate Two," Top replied to the electronic summons.

"Checkmate Two, this is Checkmate," Ray said. "Things have ground to a halt over at Checkmate Three. Send one rifle section and a machine gun crew over to take some of the pressure off that sector. Out."

Top bellowed over at his ARVN counterpart, Chief Sergeant Quan. "Hao! Take a rifle section and one of the machine guns over to the Third Commando. They're bogged down."

112

"Yes!" Quan yelled back. He quickly tagged a section leader and motioned to one of the .30-caliber Browning crews. "Di theo toi!" he ordered.

The little relief force, laying down its own covering fire, slugged its way through the reeling NVA forces. When they reached Malpractice, the Black Eagle quickly directed them to lay down fire where he needed some more pressure taken off his boys. Within fifteen minutes, Quan and his group were blasting fusillades into the enemy line.

"Checkmate," Malpractice radioed back after a quarter of an hour of the effort. "We're in good shape now. I can move forward again."

"Roger," Ray Swift Elk replied. Then he transmitted to the entire force. "All Checkmates! We have to link up with Falconi and the guys or they'll be goners. Push! Push! Push!"

In his firing position at the edge of the enemy mortar battery, Archie Dobbs spotted three NVA riflemen moving toward him. He raised the muzzle of his M16 and took quick sight pictures. He pulled the trigger three times but only two shots erupted from the weapon. Both cut down an enemy soldier each, but the third Red, wide-eyed with rage, charged toward the Black Eagle.

Archie faked a shot with his now empty rifle then leaped up and charged forward with his bayonet fixed. He and the NVA closed in and made jabs at each other. The blades of the stabbing weapons clanked as they parried and thrust, both men's faces masks of grim determination. The enemy soldier, suddenly remembering he still had a loaded weapon, jerked on the trigger. The round whipped past Archie's ear and the Black Eagle desperately lunged with his bayonet. He missed the soldier but got the blade under the man's rifle sling.

"Yah!" Archie yelled, pulling back and yanking the weapon from the man's hand. Unfortunately, he lost the

113

grip on his own and both rifles sailed off into the air, somersaulting into the bushes. The two combatants leaped at each other, clawing, kicking, cursing, and snarling.

The NVA kicked at Archie's shins landing bruising blows on the American's lower legs. Now really pissed off, Archie managed to get his hands around the other's throat. Each stab of pain added to his fury, and his grip tightened until the Red suddenly weakened, his tongue sticking out as his eyes rolled upward.

The moment Archie dropped the body, more MVA appeared. He made a running dive for his M16, desperately clawing at his ammo pouch. At that moment Blue joined him.

"Put a grenade in the middle o' them bastards!" Archie yelled as he slammed a fresh magazine into his rifle.

Blue complied and blew away three of the attackers. But more appeared. He and Archie settled down to trade shots with them.

"Where the fuck is the battalion?" Archie demanded to know as he fired into a growing crowd of attacking enemy infantry. "If they ain't here pretty damned quick we're gone goslings, baby!"

Back on the other side of the perimeter, Falconi and Paulo Garcia had formed an impromptu fighting team. Incoming rounds were numerous and pocked the trees around them as the pair blasted away at the attackers, trying to hold them at bay.

Gunnar Olson suddenly dove in between them. Wordlessly, he raised his M203 and cut loose with an M576 buckshot canister. He quickly followed this with two more, forcing the enemy assault to momentarily melt back into the jungle.

Now Archie and Blue rushed back into the area. They flopped down and joined in the crashing volleys of the others. "Lots o' pressure coming in now, sir," Archie announced. "We got to get relieved and damned quick."

"Yeah," Falconi said between pumping rounds at the

enemy. "Come on, Ray, baby! We need you—*now!*"

The last of Calvin Culpepper's barrage had dwindled into distant echoes. Ray Swift Elk ordered the entire battalion through the dead zone the heavy shower of shells had created. The rangers leaped over their own casualties, intermingled with the enemy's, as they moved forward in ragged but determined skirmish lines.

Small-arms fire increasd dramatically as the attackers moved into the NVA's secondary line of resistance. There were solid positions there, even better prepared than those on the MLR. Captain Ray Swift Elk had expected that. His strategically placed machine gun squads now opened up, their positioning giving them uninterrupted fields of fire across the entire FEBA. Rifle sections laid down bases of fire to allow others to move in closer, but the enemy was sitting tight and prepared. They fought back tenaciously, their own salvos of fire whipping through the ARVN troops.

After five minutes of heartbreaking effort on both sides, the battle hit a stalemate. Attackers and defenders were locked into a stubborn slugfest.

And Falconi and the infiltrators still waited.

Chapter 12

Falconi surveyed the scene to his direct front. His men, spread out along the precarious perimeter of their defensive position, did their best to cover their battle front while crouching in positions formerly occupied by NVA infantry.

It was most assuredly not a period of relaxation. The time passed with tension and excitement as small units of the enemy made what seemed to be independent but frequent attacks on the Black Eagles. They would suddenly appear and open fire, throwing in blasting sprays of slugs. Then, just as quickly, they ducked out of sight, only to hit again at another section of the line. Their tactics were more difficult to handle than an all-out frontal assault. The Black Eagles felt like the wolf being bitten to death by fleas. Scratch and bite in one place only to be suddenly bitten in another.

"Steve!" Falconi yelled. He spotted a team of enemy riflemen making another sneaky move. "Shift your fire to the right!"

Steve Matsuno swung the muzzle of his M16, spewing out a swarm of full-auto fire. He knocked over two NVA before their buddies dove to cover and disappeared.

"That'll learn 'em, dern 'em!" Steve yelled.

Falconi checked his watch. It was only a matter of time before the NVA really got their nerve up and came storming into the area like gangbusters. If Ray Swift Elk didn't push through to link up with him pretty soon, the small parachute assault force would be overwhelmed.

Firing suddenly erupted on the far right. Paulo Garcia's voice could barely be heard above the roaring gunfire. "They're trying to outflank us!"

Falconi quickly went into action. He turned toward Loco Padilla's fire team, hollering as loud as he could. "Archie! Blue! Come with me!"

The pair leaped up and ran to join him. Then all three Black Eagles sprinted across the middle of the mortar area. They dove behind a pile of sandbags that had been the NVA mortar commander's simple command post.

"Put in support fire over there. Just above Gunnar's head," Falconi ordered. Then he added, "Try not to hit him, okay?"

"If you insist, sir," Blue called out.

Archie on semi-auto and Blue on full-auto fired ear-splitting salvos in the direction indicated. Gunnar, to their front, instinctively ducked down behind his own sandbags as the bullets whapped through the air above him. Although he hadn't been aware of what had happened, he instinctively figured out that support fire was being thrown his way. And Gunnar knew exactly what the situation called for.

The Norwegian-American loaded his M203 with M433 rounds and began firing blindly. But a combination of experience and instinct aided him in accurately gauging the correct elevation to hold the weapon.

The Red soldiers trying to outflank the position were caught in the open. Shards of shrapnel and steel-jacketed slugs sliced through them, knocking them tumbling to the ground in shuddering heaps. Their surviving pals, moving backward rapidly, returned fire and disappeared back into cover.

"Flank is secured!" Gunnar yelled.

"Okay, you two," Falconi said to his companions. "Back to your own fire team."

117

"You bet, sir!" Archie said. "Anytime you need us. Just call."

"Don't worry, I will," Falconi said. "Now snap it up and get back to your team."

Archie and Blue raced back across the expanse of open ground to rejoin Loco Padilla and Trang Ngo. Loco directed them to different positions. "Keep your eyes open," he cautioned them. "The bastards are coming at us from ever'where!"

Falconi once more checked his watch. "C'mon, Ray. We need you, baby!" he said to himself under his breath.

The ARVN rangers and their NVA foes remained locked in bitter combat. They fought at close quarters in the confines of the jungle as each sought to blast the other off their respective line. The concussion of the continuous firing blew the leaves off trees. Many of the combatants were almost deaf; blood seeped from their ears as the invisible buffeting went on unabated.

Small gains would be made from time to time, but these were quickly lost as the attacking ARVN rangers were pushed back in a fierce exchange of gunfire and tossed grenades. The machine gunners performed heroic deeds as they raced from trouble spot to trouble spot, throwing in needed support fire to break deadlocks where the bellowing fighters were bogged down.

But such advantages gained were only short-lived.

As Swift Elk took in reports from his line commanders, he could see what was happening. The overall coordinated battle plan was breaking down into bits and pieces. Units as small as three-man fire teams, and even entire companies, were operating independently from the main group.

If the trend continued the battle would turn into a melee, with no overall gains possible. That would mean no breakthrough to link up with Falconi.

"All Checkmates," Swift Elk called over the radio. "I

say again. All Checkmates. On my command break contact with the enemy and withdraw two-five meters. Make ready." The Sioux officer waited for a full minute to give the commando leaders time to radio down to platoon and squad level. Then he pressed the transmit button on the headset. "Break! Break! Goddamn you! *Break!*"

A flurry of salvos and volleys built up then quickly settled down to sporadic firing. Impatient and irritated, Swift Elk waited by his radio. Things were far behind schedule, and getting back on track was going to be difficult if not downright impossible.

"This is Checkmate One," Captain Huy reported in. He had taken command of the First Assault Commando when Swift Elk moved into Falconi's position. "We have made move and contact is broken."

"This is Checkmate Two," came Sergeant Major Top Gordon's voice. "We're backed off and holding."

Malpractice McCorckel did not waste words. "Checkmate Three clear."

"All Checkmates! Attack!. Attack! Hit 'em, you bastards!" Swift Elk commanded.

If the leaders were surprised by the flip-flop, it didn't slow them down. Firing immediately built up as the entire battalion leaped forward and smashed into the NVA.

This time the effort was coordinated and connected, with all units working in cohesion.

This was exactly what Ray wanted in his scheme to break up the little fights and once more combine his unit into one great big ass-kicking battle group. The NVA, caught unaware and confused, reeled back from the bullets, grenades, and bayonets that crashed their wavering second line of resistance.

The resurgence of fighting was so loud and explosive that Falconi and the men with him could hear it back in the NVA mortar position. Archie Dobbs, taking a drink from his canteen, glanced over at the commanding officer.

"Looks like the big push is on, sir."

"Yeah," Falconi agreed. "And not too soon to suit me."

Archie grinned. Forever the optimist, he laughed. "Ol' Ray is gonna clean them NVAs' clock for 'em, all right!"

The uproar was so great that the reserve company of enemy infantry had been pulled back. The report of the incident was brought in by Steve Matsuno, who occupied the most forward fighting position.

"They're gone for now, sir," he said squatting down beside the colonel. "I'm sure they'll be back, but the bastards have pulled away from our perimeter. I suppose they're standing by in case Swift Elk and the rest of the commandos break through."

"That's a damned good assumption," Falconi said. "And it's time to get this show on the road now."

"All or nothing, Colonel Falconi?" Blue Richards asked.

"All or nothing," Falconi replied. "And now I've got a chance to put our real reason for being here to work."

The Black Eagle commander reached back in his patrol pack and pulled out the first of the thermite grenades he had been carrying. Working rapidly, he went from mortar to mortar and dropped one of the fiery devices down the tube after pulling the pin.

The grenades, designed to burn for forty seconds, lit off at a temperature of no less than 4,300 degrees after the thermite filler in the interior changed to molten iron. The awful heat fused, welded, and burned holes in the heavy weapons, turning them into twisted hunks of useless metal.

When the chore was finished, he gathered the parachute infiltrators around him. "Okay, boys, you've heard me say this before and you're going to hear it again. It is now do-or-die time. I'm not sure what's happening up on the front lines, but it's a certainty the situation isn't going to improve."

"So what's on the agenda?" Archie asked.

"If Swift Elk can't link up with us," Falconi said, "then we'll link up with him."

"How the hell are we gonna do that, sir?" Loco Padilla asked. "There's a whole goddamned battalion of NVA between us and him."

"We'll form into a double column with a fire team on each side," Falconi explained. "Since the enemy situation is fluid and uncertain we can slice through them like the proverbial hot knife through butter."

"We can?" Paulo Garcia asked. "I hope you're right about that, sir."

"Yeah," Loco said. "If we stall, we're cooked gooses."

"So you realize that we must. And I say again—we *must!*" Falconi emphasized. "So let's knock off the bullshit and get moving. Alphas on the left and Bravos on the right. Form up and prepare to move out."

In less than sixty seconds the group was in the proper formation, with Falconi between the two fire teams. Falconi looked around and gave the old-fashioned thumbs-up signal. The men responded with winks and grins. "Okay! Go!" the colonel shouted.

They charged straight out of the mortar area and crashed into the jungle. After traveling only a few meters they ran straight into a rifle section left back to contain them.

Blue and Gunnar, their M203 grenade launchers primed and ready, rushed to the front. The NVA soldiers, concealed but not protected by jungle brush, set up quick defensive fusillades that swept across the Black Eagle column. The two grenadiers fired simultaneously, sending a blasting swarm of buckshot flying into the enemy position. The defenders were shredded by the terrible weapons unleashed at such short range. Too busy and occupied to cheer, Falconi and his men charged over the stacked, torn cadavers.

Suddenly an enemy machine gun swept rapid fire at them from the right front. Their forward progress came to an abrupt halt and the men hit the dirt as the air around them filled with flying 7.62-millimeter slugs. Archie Dobbs, the farthest forward, rolled over on his back and pulled a fragmentation grenade from his harness. After pulling the pin he tossed it with a sweeping but inaccurate throw.

The explosive device hit a tree and bounced back landing beside Paulo Garcia. Cursing, the marine frantically grabbed the grenade and flung it in the direction of the machine gun. It exploded in the air, doing no damage to the enemy.

"Thanks a lot, Archie, you asshole!" he angrily yelled. "If I'd been a second or two slower, I'd been dead meat!"

Archie, sorely embarrassed, could only wince.

Gunnar, taking a chance, leaped up and fired an M433 round from his grenade launcher. But it simply ricocheted off a couple of trees and detonated harmlessly as the Norwegian-American ducked back down to the ground.

More machine gun fire came in with increasing bursts of bullets. It was closer now, and the Black Eagles hugged the ground while tracer ammo hissed inches above their heads.

Gunnar decided to try again.

This time he tried an airburst M397 grenade. He waited for a brief lull in the incoming fire, then came up on his knees and shot the weapon with frantic quickness before ducking back down.

The round zipped toward the machine gun. It hit a tree trunk and the small charge inside went off throwing it five feet higher. When the main round exploded, it blew its full force of concussion and steel at the machine gun. The weapon was swept over on its side and the unfortunate crew were gashed to bloody hunks by the flying shrapnel.

"On your feet!" Falconi commanded. "Move out!"

The two fire teams instantly obeyed and charged out of the hell hole where they had been pinned down. Running rapidly, they headed straight toward the battle ahead of them. But as soon as they broke through a particularly thick stand of jungle vegetation and into a glen, they were once more confronted by a determined group of enemy.

This time it was the rest of the riflemen who had contained them back at the mortar area.

The clearing was small and everyone had trouble trying to maneuver in the confined space. The Black Eagles, following instincts built up through countless battles, simply charged straight ahead, bowling into the midst of the NVA position.

Loco Padilla was the first to make contact. He threw a horizontal butt stroke that hit an enemy rifleman so hard his helmet flew off as the man went down. Archie, almost bumping into Loco, got off a quick shot that blew off another Red's face.

The enemy was also firing, and one round hit Archie's jacket collar. The force of the impact spun him completely around leaving him a bit dazed and plenty dizzy. Blue, unable to bring up his own M16, noted the NVA was going to shoot at Archie again. He took two long strides forward and drove the heel of his hand in the Red's jaw, snapping the soldier's head back. Trang Ngo brought the little episode to a final conclusion by pumping three shots into the NVA's torso. He spun on his heel and fired again, this time knocking two more of the enemy onto the ground.

While that was going on, the Bravo Fire Team had completely blown away that side of the line. But there was no time to celebrate the violent victory. At Falconi's urging, the column moved forward, reaching a point between the NVA's newly established Main Line of Resistance and their Second Line of Resistance.

The advantage of the situation was that the NVA on the MLR did not know Falconi and his men were there. The disadvantage—and it was a hell of a handicap—came

123

from the fact that the enemy on the SLR fired straight into the Black Eagles' backs.

Falconi did not find it necessary to issue orders at that point in the dangerous proceedings. Everybody in both fire teams went like hell.

They crashed into the back of the Reds' MLR, sweeping swarms of bullets ahead of them. Some of the enemy, noting the new direction of incoming fire, immediately turned to resist, but they died quick.

Blue and Gunnar kept firing the buckshot canisters at regular intervals, blowing wider and wider holes in the Reds. For a moment—one shining, blasting, bloody moment—it looked like they might make it.

But an enemy reserve force came in from the side. This new group, heavy with automatic weapons and grenades, threw everything they had at Falconi's column. The Black Eagle momentum sagged, then halted.

The breakthrough attempt had failed.

The colonel took his men back through a devastated area of the NVA Secondary Line of Resistance. The pressure from their pursuers was so great that they finally returned to the glen, forced to take cover amidst the bodies of the NVA they had killed only moments before.

Archie checked his dwindling ammo supply. "I don't think this is called progress," he remarked to Blue beside him.

"Nope," Blue said shaking his head. "I believe what we're doin' is popularly known as spinnin' yer wheels."

Trang Ngo was more direct. He spat. "Here we die!"

Even Archie's spirits finally sagged. "Goddamn it! We didn't pull it off!"

Ngo repeated to himself. "Here we die!"

Chapter 13

Captain Cuong Ngoi of the NVA unit had been kept extremely busy during the battle. Aside from his duties as deputy commander of the battalion, he was also charged with supply responsibilities. That meant he was constantly overseeing the distribution of ammunition and rations where and when they were needed. And all this amid the blasting turmoil of constant combat.

These duties required that the captain also keep a mental SITREP running through his mind. There was no excuse for not keeping tabs on things or for forgetting detail, because when Major Tanh Hyun demanded information on the current situation, he wanted it accurate and up to date.

Ngoi employed a noncommissioned officer as information gatherer, and he was glad when the sergeant finally brought him not only interesting but happy intelligence on the battle's circumstances. Ngoi wasted no time in rushing to the battalion command post.

When he reported to his commanding officer, he had to shout because of the noise of the fighting going on around them. "Comrade Major!" he hollered. "We have the infiltrators trapped in the clearing where the reserve section was located when they were wiped out."

"Ah!" Major Hyun said. "Then the cursed enemy skulkers who slaughtered our brave comrades there did not break through?"

Ngoi shook his head. "The comrades at the front line held them up until the second reserve section was able to move in. A fierce battle raged there for a bit, but our soldiers prevailed," the captain reported. He liked to embellish things when he knew it would increase the battalion commander's pleasure. "The enemy has been forced back from the MLR. When I was advised as to their exact location, I ordered in the third and fourth reserves to contain them within the bounds of that small clearing."

"Well done, Comrade Captain!" Hyun said happily. "Do not send any more riflemen to fight them. Those devils are costing us too many casualties. Instead, fetch one of the recoilless rifle crews. The overall tactical situation does not require their presence and they will be able to deal quite handily with the infiltrators." He chuckled. "The recoilless riflemen will not suffer like the men of the regular sections."

"I will order them to the scene," the captain said. "A section will be in action against the infiltrators within a quarter hour, Comrade Major!"

He saluted and rushed back toward the rear, where the NVA battalion's recoilless rifle platoon had set up an emergency perimeter to cover any withdrawals from the front. Ngoi didn't bother with protocol under the circumstances. Bypassing the unit's commander, he simply ran up to the nearest crew and gave them terse orders to pick up their weapon and crates of ammunition and follow him. They did so immediately, trotting after the officer as they rushed as fast as possible into the jungle under their heavy burdens.

Finally Ngoi stopped. An NCO in charge of reserve riflemen guarding the clearing hurried forward.

"The enemy is still contained, Comrade Captain," he reported. "They are only firing when we expose ourselves to them."

"Then the running dogs have made no effort to break

out?" Ngoi asked.

"No, Comrade Captain," the veteran sergeant replied. "Perhaps they are growing low on ammunition."

"Duoc roi!" Captain Ngoi exclaimed. "That would make sense. They could not have brought much with them." He turned to the senior gunner of the recoilless rifle crew. "There are enemy infiltrators in a small clearing straight ahead," he said pointing in the indicated direction.

The crew chief, another seasoned fighter, nodded. "Do you know the range, Comrade Captain?"

Ngoi smiled. "Less than twenty-five meters. If it wasn't for the fighting going on nearby you would be able to hear them breathing." He laughed. "Or should I say weeping?"

"Do we wish to take prisoners, Comrade Captain?"

"The orders are to destroy the bastards!" Ngoi hissed. "Nothing less will please the comrade major."

The crew chief chuckled and patted his awesome weapon. "We will fire with a level tube, Comrade Major. What our shrapnel misses, the hunks of trees and rocks kicked up by concussion will do the rest."

"Carry on, Comrade Gunner!" Ngoi urged him.

The crew chief turned toward his crewmen and barked, "Di ra! Set up the gun!" He pointed to a spot on the ground.

The man with the heavy tripod trotted forward and dropped the implement to the dirt. He was followed instantly by a man carrying the barrel-and-receiver group, who quickly and expertly clamped it into place.

Now the crew chief went into action. He placed the sight into its correct slot on the side of the receiver. "Load the spotter round!"

An ammunition bearer stepped forward and put a 12.7-millimeter tracer bullet in the gun barrel that lay across the top of the tube. "Spotter round loaded, Comrade Sergeant!" he reported.

After sighting where he wanted to fire, the crew chief

pulled the trigger. The single round went off, streaking into the jungle. He carefully noted what location and height it entered the thick vegetation to his direct front.

After adjustments, the NCO again ordered, "Load the spotter round!" When that was accomplished, he fired again. "On target!" he reported. "Load, one round, high explosive!"

Another ammo man came forward. Well-drilled and practiced, he shoved a large shell into the breach. He slammed it shut and patted the crew chief on the head. He quickly leaped to the side since the entire recoil of the weapon blew out the back and would blow anything—or anyone—within a distance of fifteen meters to the rear into pieces.

The sergeant pressed the trigger. This time a deafening roar exploded over the scene and the shell streaked toward the area concealing Colonel Robert Falconi and his team of parachute infiltrators.

The situation out on the battle front remained the same. Casualties among the combatants had been extremely heavy, but the fighting continued unabated.

The NVA main line of resistance, mauled and shattered, managed to hold together through the efforts of the small unit leaders—the lieutenants and sergeants—as the ARVN ranger commandos, led by the Black Eagles, slammed into them in relentless fury.

The swirling nature of the battle that ebbed back and forth through the jungle left dead of both sides intermingled and even piled on top of each other. More than humans suffered from the flying slugs and shrapnel. Even the rain forest's terrain had paid a terrible price in the fighting. Large sections of the lush jungle had been splintered and blown down. Stands of bamboo, groves of khoai-sap, and even the tallest of tamarind tres were smashed to the ground as if by a large, swatting hand. In some places, the damaged vegetation covered the bodies

128

of dead soldiers killed in earlier fighting.

Captain Ray Swift Elk was close to total exhaustion. He had been without any rest or sleep for thirty-six straight hours. No less than three radio operators had collapsed trying to keep up with the Sioux Indian officer as he tirelessly went from hot spot to hot spot, personally directing the deadly flurries of attack, defense, and counterattack as the hammering against the NVA continued unabated. Swift Elk's great experience in combat command came to the fore as he solved problems, cooled off hot spots, and made instantaneous decisions to remedy situations gone bad.

Now, the fourth ARVN radio operator assigned to him trotted obediently after the Black Eagle officer as he continued urging his command to pound their way forward in the desperate effort to link up with Falconi and the remainder of the parachute infiltrators.

Up in the Second Assault Commando, Sergeant Major Top Gordon supervised his unit's attacks, sometimes leading charges himself. But in spite of Top's best efforts, the elusive North Vietnamese continued their fluid defense of fire, retreat and maneuver, then counterattack. The senior noncommissioned officer had made one late afternoon attack and had been forced to stubbornly withdraw as he and his men exchanged small-arms fire with the fiercely obstinate Red soldiers.

Any other unit commander would have seriously considered breaking all contact with the enemy and giving his men a complete rest. But there were limits to the sergeant major's conception of retreat.

Top pulled back only the necessary amount to set up his own defense and was joined by Swift Elk, who was trooping the line.

"We keep bouncing off 'em, sir," Top reported.

"How's your unit strength?" Swift Elk asked.

"We're down fifty percent now," Top answered. He studied the captain's face, noting his red-rimmed eyes. "Sir, you're close to falling flat on your ass."

129

"I like your delicate way of putting things," Swift Elk said with a weak grin.

"You got to take a coupla hours off," Top said.

"The colonel and the guys are still out there someplace," Swift Elk said. "We got to make that link-up."

"Hell, yes, we got to!" Top snapped. "We all know that and we're doing our best. You're doing your best. But you driving yourself 'til you drop ain't gonna give us any relief, is it?"

"I can't let anything slip past me," Swift Elk insisted.

"You'll find out when you're needed, Cap'n," Top said. "Take a break, goddamn it! This here fight isn't going our way as it is!"

"Then I'll make it go our way!" Swift Elk snapped.

"Face up to it, Cap'n!" Top said. "We're at a standstill here. We can't whip them and they can't whip us." Top's own fatigue was taking its toll. "Why the fuck don't you lighten up before you fall over?!"

Swift Elk bellowed, "Stop chewing my ass, Sergeant Major! Now get off your frigging keester and take those troops of yours forward again. And keep doing it until every damned one of you is dead!"

"Yes, sir! That'll be in about another half hour!" Top yelled back. His hot flash of temper wiped away any coolness of judgement he had left after the long exposure to combat. He pivoted and rushed back to his depleted rifle squads. "On your feet, you brawling bastards, and follow me! We're going up there and we ain't coming back!"

Swift Elk also took action. He grabbed the handset from his radioman. "All Checkmates! I want an attack all along the line. And I mean the *entire* fucking line! *Now!*"

Recoilless rifle shells plowed into the area occupied by Colonel Robert Falconi and his band of parachute infiltrators. They hugged the ground and clasped their hands over their ears as the blasting detonations roared around them, kicking up thick clouds of dust and throwing debris such as rocks and broken twigs through the air. Even worse, bodies of the dead NVA that lay sprawled where they had fallen throughout the area were ripped apart by the incoming fire. Hunks of their flesh and speckles of coagulated blood fell on the huddled defenders in the glen.

At times the concussion lifted some of the Black Eagles off the ground and they fell back heavily, getting the breath knocked out of them. Spitting dirt and sweating profusely, they endured the pounding as best they could.

Falconi, as battered and buffeted as his men, tried to keep himself oriented. His eyes stung from the dust blown into them and his face was peppered with pebbles and hunks of earth. In spite of the physical punishment, the colonel kept himself calm, ready to react at the first opportunity that presented itself for positive action.

From all indications there were still riflemen outside the clearing covering them. He could tell from the direction and amount of shells blasting into the middle of the perimeter that there was a single recoilless rifle firing at them. Luckily—if this could be called luck—the Black Eagles were in a small depression. If the ground had been flat there wouldn't be a hunk bigger than a bread box left of any of them.

Falconi knew, however, that as more time passed the incoming shells would eventually inflict casualties on his small, separated command. The ground, already plowed and torn up, was fast deteriorating. It was time to make a move. He tried to yell orders, but could not be heard above the explosions of 57-millimeter shells that blasted into their position.

Falconi suddenly remembered two maxims from his days at Infantry Officers Candidate School at Fort Benning. The first was *"Do something, even if it's not right,"* and, much more important, *"Lead by example."*

The colonel decided to follow those lessons learned early in his military career.

He waited for another of the recoilless rifle explosions. When it went off, he was rolled over by the blast. He continued the maneuver until he was back on his stomach. Then he leaped up and charged forward, swinging the muzzle of his M16 back and forth as he fired on full automatic.

The first man to see him was Archie Dobbs. After serving with Falconi for so much time, he knew exactly what the "Old Man" was up to. Archie leaped up, also firing straight ahead. Then Blue and Gunnar joined them, holding their M203 grenade launchers locked and loaded, ready for action. In less than a couple of beats the other five men followed suit. Damning common sense, damning any semblance of instinct for survival, damning even the fear they felt, the entire parachute infiltration team raced yelling and shooting at the enemy that surrounded them.

Back at the recoilless rifle, the crew chief prepared to fire again. He put his eye to the sight and was astounded to see that his intended victims had burst out of the clearing and were charging straight at him. He stared at them for one incredulous second before a single round hit him in the forehead. His skull cracked open in the back as brains and bloody goo blew out. The dead man remained sitting. He didn't even topple over.

Gunnar and Blue once again employed buckshot from the M203s to clear a path for the detachment. Most of the flying balls of buckshot hit the recoilless rifle crew, splattering them all over their crates of ammunition still waiting to be fired. When Gunnar reached the weapon, he kicked the dead crew chief aside and pulled it out of the tripod. Hefting it up on his shoulder, he fired the still loaded recoilless rifle straight into the enemy riflemen farther back.

The 57-millimeter round exploded, killing several riflemen and Captain Cuong Ngoi. All were blown to bits. The captain's days of sweating Major Hyun's rages had ended forever.

Falconi immediately recognized the great opportunity that had presented itself with Gunnar's seizure of the heavy weapon. "Ky! Ngoi!" he shouted. "Get ammo and follow Gunnar!"

Each of the Vietnamese picked up satchels of 57-millimeter shells and ran after the Norwegian-American, who had adopted the Chicom weapon as his own.

With the addition of the recoilless rifle, the breakout was renewed with extra strength. Gunnar's expertise with heavy weaponry meant they now had their own fire support. Between that and Blue's M203, the Black Eagles knocked down any more resistance and roared through the NVA secondary line of resistance, blasting a good size hole like a team of NFL linemen opening up the opposition's defense for a running back.

As they crossed the open space between the secondary and main lines of resistance, they took in small arms fire. Blue, changing over to airbursts, sent out deadly sprays of shrapnel over the heads of the NVA. The white-hot hunks of deadly metal splattered any enemy rifleman within range into a bloody, torn corpse.

Falconi led his men out of the enemy line and into no-man's land between the two forces. Now the fire directed at them increased in activity and they were forced to turn and move backward, trading shot for shot with the NVA filling in the hole they'd left.

Gunnar used the last three rounds of the recoilless rifle to advantage, reopening the enemy line with each carefully aimed shell. He had just fired the last one when Archie grabbed his belt and roughly jerked him backward for several meters.

"C'mon!" Archie yelled. "You're forgetting we're supposed to be moving to our own lines."

Things again slipped into limbo for a moment as the NVA firepower suddenly leaped in volume. For a brief instant it appeared that the infiltrators' escape might bog down. But Top Gordon and his Second Assault Commando came up on line and added their support. The

133

combined firepower forced the NVA back. Now linked up, parachute infiltrators and ARVN rangers turned and made a break for their own side of the battlefield.

When they arrived in friendly territory, Falconi and his team stumbled back from the MLR. Emotionally and physically wrung out, they allowed themselves the luxury of taking a ten-minute break. They gave each other silent nods of congratulations. The mission had been accomplished: the enemy mortars, ruined by the thermite grenades, were out of order.

Falconi got to his feet. He knew he couldn't waste any more time. Somewhere Ray Swift Elk was still running the battle without knowing the infiltration team had made it back.

He yelled over at Top, "Send me a radio!" He glanced down at his men still resting. "Hey, goddamn it! Let's get back to work. We've still got this campaign to win."

Chapter 14

Captain Ray Swift Elk had never been so happy to see Falconi in his life. Not only did he know his friend and commander was safe, along with the infiltration team, but the pressure was off him for a while.

After meeting the colonel and turning overall leadership back to him, Swift Elk finally allowed himself to relax. But not before giving his commanding officer a full report on what had been going on between the jump and the final link-up.

"Well done, Ray," Falconi said.

"I'm not real satisfied, sir," Swift Elk replied. "I was hoping like hell to break through and make the get-together on the enemy's side of the front lines."

"Yeah, me too," Falconi said. "If we'd have pulled it off this operation would be wrapped up nice and proper. No doubt about that."

"What about the NVA, sir?" Swift Elk asked. "What's their strength and status over there?"

"They're a hell of a lot stronger than we thought they were," Falconi told him. "Frankly, I gave you an impossible task without knowing it. But now that the NVA's mortars are neutralized and we can put ours into effect, I think we can wrap up this campaign in short time."

Ray grinned. "I was really tempted to have Calvin

really cut loose with his 81s. But in order to make it effective enough for us to break down the enemy MLR, he would have blown you and the other guys over there to Kingdom Come."

"Captain, I appreciate your patience and equanimity," Falconi said with a grin. "Now get some rest. You really need it, Ray."

"Yes, sir."

The Sioux snapped a salute and walked over to a comfortable spot beneath a surviving sugar apple tree. He spread out his poncho liner for his bed and his patrol pack for a pillow. Then he lay down, closed his eyes, and sank into a deep, dreamless slumber.

Falconi waited until his deputy commander was fast asleep before he called a staff meeting. He knew if he held any planning sessions, Swift Elk would insist on participating, even if he were totally exhausted. Paulo Garcia, the second-in-command of the First Assault Commando, represented the unit leader. He could fill Ray Swift Elk in on all the juicy details of Falconi's plans later.

Everyone gathered around the colonel's command post, which was no more than the spot under a soursop tree where he threw down his gear and made himself comfortable. Colonel Long Kuyen, Sergeant Major Top Gordon, Master Sergeant Malpractice McCorckel, Chief Warrant Officer Calvin Culpepper, Sergeant Loco Padilla, and the rest of the Goon team gathered around their commander.

Top, whose Third Assault Commando had borne the brunt of the fighting, raised his hand. "Are we gonna attack again, sir?"

"Our men are too worn out for the time being," Falconi said. "Particularly yours, Top."

"Yes, sir," Malpractice agreed. Then he pointed out, "So's the enemy, Colonel. They ain't exactly dancing the fandango over there."

"Right," Paulo Garcia said. "It's kind of like a toss-up, ain't it?"

"Not exactly," Falconi cautioned him. "You must remember that the attacker is always at a greater disadvantage than the defender. If we hit their line, the NVA could fight us without moving around too much. We, on the other hand, would be firing and maneuvering like crazy while we tried to force our way through their positions."

"You're right, sir," Top said. "We'd never make it now."

"At least we knocked out the bastards' mortars," Loco pointed out.

"Yeah," Falconi said. "Those thermite grenades sure as hell bring hot scalding pee."

"So what's on our agenda?" Calvin Culpepper asked.

"The first thing I want is a report from the commandos," Falconi said.

Paulo Garcia was the first to sound off. "I checked things out when we got back from the infiltration. Morale is pretty good and that's a surprise to me."

Colonel Kuyen smiled. "No surprise, Sergeant. Our men have been defeated and driven away at every battle before. Now they have stuck it out and have even pushed the enemy back a bit. We may be at a stalemate, but that is almost as good as a victory to my brave rangers."

"Good point," Falconi said. "And I must compliment Colonel Kuyen and his rangers. It has been a proud experience to fight alongside them."

"I am honored, Colonel Falconi," the ARVN officer said.

Falconi glanced over at Sergeant Major Top Gordon. "How're things over in the Second Commando?"

"We're down fifty percent," Top said. "My men are wrung out but still willing to fight."

"Same with my outfit," Malpractice said. "Except we're better off in numbers than Top. We haven't taken that many hits. I estimate that we're between sixty and seventy percent strength. But we've still lost a lot of men."

"Will your guys continue the good fight?" Falconi asked.

"Damn right, sir!"

Falconi gave Calvin Culpepper a playful nudge. "What about you, Mister Culpepper?" He addressed the warrant officer in the proper manner for his rank.

"Hell! We're bad and sassy," Calvin said. "We ain't taken no hits and—I'm real sorry to say, guys—we ain't done too much to help out."

"Don't worry about it," Falconi said. "If Swift Elk had called you in full bore, you'd have blown the hell out of me and the others over there, too."

"Yeah," Calvin said sadly. "It seems I'm damned if I do and damned if I don't."

"Cheer up, Calvin," Falconi said. "You'll get your chance."

"I'm waiting for that, sir," Calvin said. "My big question is, when do I get my turn on the dance floor?"

"I'm going to let twenty-four hours slide by," Falconi said. "There're several reasons for that. First and most important, the men." He pointed to himself and the others at the meeting. "We, too, are in need of a damned good rest. We've got to catch our breaths, guys, or we'll slowly but surely slip straight down those proverbial tubes."

"That seems like a long time, sir," Top said.

"In a way that'll be good," Falconi said. "From what we saw during our parachute infiltration, the North Vietnamese are stunned. The bastards are waiting to see what we're going to do. If we sit still for that long they won't know whether to shit or go blind. It might even provoke an attack out of them."

"And my mortars are ready!" Calvin exclaimed.

"Great," Falconi said. "In the meantime, go back to your units and check them out. If you see any problems, let me know. Reassure your guys that the situation is well in hand. Keep them on the alert and tell them to rest up. Emphasize that this operation is closing down. But the

138

ending is going to be like a Fourth of July fireworks' display—fiery, noisy, and wild as hell. And when the smoke and the fire cools down, it's going to be a god-damned victory. A complete, unadulterated, goddamned victory!"

Archie Dobbs's voice came from the back of the crowd. "Or we'll all be dead and gone."

"Worried, Archie?" Falconi called out.

"Me, sir? Adversity spurs me on," Archie said. Then he laughed. "I've had a lot of spurs dug into my ass in this unit, believe me!"

They were suddenly interrupted by Steve Matsuno, who appeared from the front lines with a prisoner in tow. The man, wearing the collar insignia of a junior non-commissioned officer, smiled and bobbed his head in a typical Asian show of humility and respect.

"What the hell do you have there, Steve?" Falconi asked standing up.

"A deserter, sir," Steve said. "He showed up in front of our lines. One of the rangers damned near shot him before I yelled out for everybody to hold their fire."

"You mean you didn't go out and capture him?" Falconi asked.

"No, sir. He came bopping over to us with his hands in the air hollering 'Durng ban!'"

Falconi grinned. "This is, indeed, a good sign. Sit him down." He fished in his pocket and pulled out a pack of cigarettes offering one to the prisoner. After lighting it for him, Falconi said, "Chao ong. Toi ten la Dai-Ta Falconi." Then he asked, "Ten ong la gi?"

"My name is Junior Sergeant Gio," the man answered in Vietnamese. "I have left my unit and come over to you voluntarily. Please, Colonel. I beg for mercy and good treatment."

"Of course," Falconi said. "Are you hungry?"

"Yes, Colonel," Gio answered. "We are short of rations. The last food I had was some mangos, two days ago."

"You have no field rations?"

Gio shook his head. "We are short of everything, Colonel. Our ammunition dwindles and there are no more medical supplies to treat the wounded. It is most difficult to bear. The fear in the men grows with each passing hour. And now we have learned that our mortars are destroyed."

Falconi displayed a wry grin. "*Co!* We know something of that."

"Without the mortars we can neither attack nor defend effectively," the prisoner said. "But our comrade leader will not surrender. We know he will insist that we fight to the death. I could see he had blundered and will sacrifice us to his own stupid pride. For that reason I decided to desert. I think you will win the war."

The men around the command post settled down to listen to Falconi continue his interrogation.

"What sort of unit do you belong to?" Falconi asked.

"We are an independent infantry battalion formed especially for this operation," Gio answered. "All our units, from the companies down to squads, are overstrength in numbers and weapons."

"Yes," Falconi said. "We determined that some time ago. How long has your unit been in this area?"

"I think four months," the prisoner answered. "We have no calendars and I tried to keep track of the days. I believe that this morning was the start of the 124th day we have been here."

"Is there any way—or contingency plan—for your unit to withdraw from here?" Falconi asked.

Junior Sergeant Gio shook his head. "No, Colonel. But even if we could escape I do not think that our comrade commander will do so. As I said, he is a fanatic. I have a friend who was posted at our battalion headquarters for a while. He told me that the comrade commander has vowed that if he cannot secure a victory on this mission then all of us will die here." Gio shrugged sadly. "There is no hope—no hope at all." He displayed an apologetic

140

look. "I am a good soldier but I do not wish to die for nothing. I want to see my home village again."

"Does your unit have problems other than rations and ammunition?" Falconi inquired. "How is the fighting spirit of your comrades."

Gio displayed a weak smile. "All but gone. With no mortars we know that another attack will wipe us out." He shuddered. "All the comrades are frightened as they wait for your next move. They know they will die."

"Very well," Falconi said. He looked over at Colonel Long Kuyen of the ARVN rangers. "I'll turn this POW over to you."

The South Vietnamese officer summoned a couple of his men, who marched the prisoner off to the rear. He sat back down beside Falconi. "Does this change your plans?"

"Most definitely," Falconi said. "It pretty well coincides with what we saw on the other side of the lines. I think the NVA are fighting more out of desperation than dedication. So I'm cutting down the waiting time from twenty-four to twelve hours. I want an all-out offensive launched."

Calvin Culpepper grinned. "I'll have those mortars primed and ready for support fire, sir."

Falconi reached over and patted his shoulder. "Sorry, Calvin. But a mortar barrage would simply announce our intentions. From what that prisoner said, I've determined that an all-out surprise attack will roll 'em up."

Calvin nodded. "Yes, sir. But I'll be ready just in case."

"That's the ticket!" Falconi said. He checked his watch. "We'll move out just after dawn. Get your commandos ready. The attack will begin by my voice command over the radio net."

The commando leaders stood up and saluted. Top grinned wryly. "Colonel, I hope that my bitching about losses don't make you think the Second Commando can't head up the middle again."

"I know better than that, Sergeant Major," Falconi said. "You guys have the honor. You can lead the breakthrough."

"You damned right we will!" Top replied.

The unit chiefs returned to their men. Although still tired and worn out from the previous fighting, the news of the POW's revelations gave their morale a real boost. The Vietnamese rangers finally saw a serious chance for victory on the horizon after all the heartbreaking fighting and dying in the past.

The tough soldiers were damned determined to charge straight through hell if necessary to smash the enemy one last time.

The battle front remained quiet as the day dragged on and evening finally settled in. Loco Padilla and Archie Dobbs were detailed to spend the night far out to the front of the MLR in no-man's land. Their job assignment was to monitor enemy activity, but mainly, they were supposed to make sure the NVA commander hadn't gone completely bonkers and was about to launch his own attack.

The two Black Eagles crawled up a bit forward of the front lines at dusk. They spotted a good place that offered concealment fifty meters away. A couple of palm trees had been blown down into a bamboo grove. Although badly chewed up, the damaged vegetation promised good concealment. When darkness came, they crawled out to the spot and prepared to spend the night observing and listening for enemy activity.

Throughout the long, dark hours, they pulled their stints of guard duty. Not a single sound came from the NVA. The enemy side of the battle front seemed to be closed down. Any casual observer would have thought the area completely deserted and empty, but the combat-developed instincts of the two observers led them to a different conclusion.

Loco and Archie knew that there were living, breathing, well-armed individuals somewhere out in that diabolical darkness.

Toward dawn the radio they had with them crackled alive. Falconi's reassuring voice came through the handset. "Oscar Papa, this is Checkmate. Over."

"This is Oscar Papa," Loco answered. "Over."

"What's the situation out there? Over."

"Like the prisoner said, the November Victor Alpha are as quiet as little mice. Over."

"Roger," Falconi transmitted back. "Keep your heads down, Oscar Papa. The shit is about to hit the fan. Out."

Both Loco and Archie hunched down in their hiding place and waited for the attack to begin. In less than two minutes firing broke out. Tracers zipped over their heads and they could hear the rounds splattering on the enemy's side of the combat zone. They heard wild yells and the entire line of rangers moved forward. In a few short moments they swept passed the observation point.

Loco and Archie were now able to stand up. As they stepped out of their hiding place, they were almost run over by a very angry Ray Swift Elk.

"What the fuck's going on around here?" the Sioux officer angrily demanded.

"The old man decided you needed a rest," Archie explained. "This here attack is supposed to wrap this operation up nice and tidy. We had a prisoner—a deserter actually—and he told us things has gone to shit over in the NVA unit."

"Give me the gory details later," Swift Elk snapped. "I have to get back to my unit and take them through this attack even if I don't know the full story."

"Don't worry, sir," Loco said. "Paulo will fill you in when you get there."

"He damned well better!" Swift Elk said rushing off.

After the captain disappeared into the jungle, Falconi and the rest of the Goons showed up. "Sir," Archie said. "Swift Elk just came by, and he was really pissed off about not being in on the attack."

"Did he seem rested?" Falconi asked.

143

·Loco laughed. "Oh, yes, sir. He was raring to go. Poor ol' Paulo Garcia is about to get his ass chewed bloody when he gets over there to the First Commando."

"Well, he won't be getting a cherry, that's for sure," Falconi said. "Come on, guys. Let's keep moving."

The attack continued without receiving any return fire. Hopeful, though a bit puzzled, the Black Eagles and rangers continued their penetration of the enemy position. They found the NVA's main line of resistance completely deserted.

"What the hell's going on?" Archie asked.

Blue Richards peered around, keeping his M16 ready for trouble. "Maybe the POW was wrong. That NVA commander might have hauled ass anyhow."

"Goddamn it!" Falconi swore. "The only real way for this operation to be wrapped up is to destroy the enemy, not let him escape."

"We can chase 'em, sir," Archie suggested.

At that moment the first enemy mortar round landed and exploded.

"What the hell?" Falconi exclaimed.

Then more shells came raining down, their detonations throwing hunks of exposed men into the air. The frequency increased until the entire front was a roaring hell of blazing explosions and flying shrapnel.

"I thought we got their goddamned mortars!" Loco yelled over the din.

"I dropped thermite grenades down their tubes!" Falconi said. He didn't have time for further comment. The entire attack broke down; men were dying by the dozen. He took the radio handset and gave quick orders. "All Checkmates! Withdraw! Out!"

The rangers broke and ran from the hell, leaving their dead and maimed strewn across the enemy's former MLR. A few tried to stop and dig in, but the incoming shells made quick work of them. The retreat continued until the entire ARVN force and the Black Eagles were back on their side of the line.

Falconi took radio reports from the commando leaders that reported all survivors had returned to occupy their old positions. The barrage crept forward toward them, then came to a stop. Casualties had been extremely high, and the surprise had hit hard at the spirit and morale of the South Vietnamese. Falconi made another radio broadcast, demanding that the deserter who gave them the information be brought to him.

When NVA Junior Sergeant Gio arrived with two guards he was laughing. "We are better supplied than you can imagine!" he said. "And our brave battalion will never retreat. We shall be here until the entire South belongs to the People's Republic of North Vietnam!"

"You're both a brave and foolish man," Falconi said coolly. "It was brave to play the role of a deserter and give us false information. Now tell me. Where did those additional mortars come from?"

"I will tell you nothing!" Gio snarled. "And I care nothing for my own life. Shoot me! You will get no information from me."

"I do not shoot prisoners," Falconi said.

Colonel Long Kuyen snapped orders at his soldiers. "We will shoot him."

"No!" Falconi exclaimed. "He has intelligence—real intelligence—that we desperately need. Have the guards take him back for a thorough interrogation."

"Yes, Colonel Falconi," Kuyen said. "I will see that the South Vietnamese G2 gets their hands on him. You Americans are sometimes too gentle."

"Suit yourself," Falconi said. He turned his attention back to the situation. "We're right back where we started."

"It was inevitable, Colonel Falconi," Kuyen reminded him. "Even if the prisoner had not appeared, we would still have had to launch an assault."

"I suppose you're right," Falconi said. "But it still

pisses me off about those mortars. I'd give a year's pay to find out where they came from."

Colonel Kuyen asked, "What are your plans now that the situation has gone to hell again."

"What they always are when I'm in a fix," Falconi calmly replied. "I shall call on the talents of Archibald Dobbs, Esquire."

Chapter 15

Falconi looked Archie straight in the eyes. "I've asked a hell of a lot out of you in the past, Archie. But never so much as I am about to do now."

The two squatted on the ground at another impromptu command post as they carried on a very informal discussion on the strategical situation they faced. The colonel did most of the talking and, from what he said, Archie sensed that the situation they were in was not unlike that of Napoleon's Imperial Guard at Waterloo. Their commander undoubtedly got them together and told the brave soldiers that something big was about to happen and some damn good men were going to die making it happen.

Archie wondered if he was going to be a one-man Imperial Guard playing to Falconi's Napoleon. He grinned, trying to lighten the situation. "Tell me the truth, sir. I'm beginning to think that your highest military goal is to get a 7.62 Kalashnikov round shot into my ass. Is that right?"

Falconi looked at him. "If it was, would you bug out on me?"

Archie swallowed and shrugged. "You know my motto where you're concerned, sir. You call, I haul, that's all!"

"I appreciate that, Archie," Falconi said seriously. "I really do." The colonel sighed. "I could use a big slug of

Fagin's Irish whiskey right now."

"Me too," Archie said. "I never seen an operation with so many ups and downs, or ins and outs, or overs and unders."

"I really have to agree with you on that one," Falconi said. "It seems we're either happy as hell or downright pissed off."

"Most of the time on other missions, things just go completely to shit and stay that way," Archie mused. "In a way, that's easier to deal with 'cause there's no way to go but straight up." He frowned. "I sure as hell thought we had 'em by the balls after we came across no-man's land."

Falconi shook his head. "I don't know where that enemy mortar fire came from. Those sons of bitches shouldn't have as much as a single operating weapon left. As far as I know, I shoved a thermite grenade down each and every tube in that damned battery."

"Yes, sir," Archie agreed. "You did. I took a look-see myself. And I can swear there wasn't another damned heavy weapon in that area."

"The NVA must have had some replacements stashed somewhere," Falconi said.

"But where?" Archie asked. "Us Goons walked through that enemy rear area like we owned the place. We seen all their supply stashes and took note of what was in 'em. There wasn't no extry mortars in the lot. Do you suppose they have some resupply activity?"

"No way," Falconi said. "This area has been heavily monitored and nothing has come in here lately but us."

"Yeah." Archie chuckled. "The Bad Luck Boys."

"At any rate, the NVA had extra mortars somewhere," Falconi said. "That wasn't our imagination awhile ago, those were real live mortar shells exploding in the middle of our happy little group."

"Which ended up not so happy."

"So," the Black Eagle commander said. "We must find out the scoop on the NVA's heavy weaponry."

148

"Yes, sir," Archie agreed. "And I know what you want. A one-man recon mission over to the enemy side with the primary mission of finding the NVA's secret stash of goodies."

"Right," Falconi said. "I would send all the Goons, but we'll never get away with an entire patrol going back there. Not any more. The NVA has been infiltrated too many times. That enemy commander is on the ball and he must be ready for more of our tricks. But in spite of that, one man—a damned good man—could pull it off."

Archie blushed a bit. "Colonel Falconi, I'll do my best for you."

"I know, Archie. You always have."

"What're my objectives, sir?"

"First, of course, is like you said. Find their hidden supply dump. Second, try to locate the new mortar battery," Falconi said. "Third, determine if we can knock it out by counter-battery fire from Calvin's detachment or if we have to call in that PBY for a bombing run."

"Either way I got to get exact map coordinates," Archie said.

"The fourth and most difficult mission is to see if you can figure out where those new mortars came from or if they simply had cached them in case of trouble," Falconi said. "I'm real suspicious right now. The NVA could have coordinated with the Viet Cong for a mini Ho Chi Minh trail into this area. The additional mortars could have been part of some contingency plan. And that might mean there are more available to the bastards."

"Maybe they got stuff stashed in tunnels, sir," Archie suggested.

"Whatever method they're using, I'll need you to check it out." Falconi checked his watch. "Since this is your show, I'm going to leave all the details up to you. What time do you want to leave?"

"After dark," Archie said. "I can get through the swamp and be in concealment by daylight. From that point on I'll work in the back of the NVA area and probe forward to find out what needs to be found out. If there are Viet Cong running a country store for the NVA, I'll dig 'em out. Don't worry, sir."

"Great. You've got time for a little shut-eye, Archie," Falconi said. "Rest up while you can."

"Yes, sir," Archie replied knowing that he probably would be awake, alert, and working for at least twenty-four hours.

"God! I hate this shit!" Chuck Fagin said.

"I am able to endure watching it because of what I've been through as a prisoner of the North," Andrea Thuy said coldly. "Their methods are cruel and unrelenting." She laughed sardonically. "This bastard has been through nothing. Nothing!"

"There is a lot of hatred in all you Vietnamese," Fagin said.

The CIA field operative and the beautiful Eurasian woman stood in the back of the darkened room. Only one bulb—a glaring 150-watter—burned in the far end of the ominous chamber. Underneath it, brightly lit by its glare, stood the North Vietnamese soldier, Junior Sergeant Gio. His body was bruised and there were burn marks where electric shocks had been applied to his skin. Gio was the one who had feigned being a deserter and infiltrated the ARVN rangers and Black Eagles' MLR in that guise.

Now, stripped naked and flanked by burly ARVN interrogators from the intelligence and security section of the hien-binh, the military police, he had endured hours of interrogation. In spite of the pressure applied to him, he had given no information.

A thin, suave ARVN captain strolled nonchalantly into the room. He walked across the length of the gloomy chamber and stopped in front of the prisoner. "I am here again, Gio. Is there anything you wish to tell me?"

"No," Gio answered. "I am thinking of the day when my victorious comrades storm into Saigon and you are

150

standing in my place and I in yours."

One of the guards struck the POW so hard that he was knocked from the light's glare. The other quickly pushed him back into view.

The captain remained unruffled. "Even if your Marx-quoting friends do come charging in here with red banners waving and shrieking their unnatural love for Ho Chi Minh, you will not be alive to participate in the celebration."

"My spirit will be here," Gio said. "That is enough for me."

"I will give you a few more moments to ponder the unhappy circumstances you are now in," the captain said. "Perhaps you will reconsider going through another cycle of questioning."

Another officer appeared in the light. He offered a cigarette to the prisoner, but it was knocked away by the first. "Why cannot I offer him this simple gift?"

The first officer snarled. "He is a despicable criminal and deserves no kindness."

The second officer turned to the prisoner. "You have proven your bravery. Why prolong the suffering? Nobody could possibly hold it against you if you talked. Everyone respects you!"

The captive spat at him.

The two officers, who had been playing the "Mutt and Jeff" game—one being severe and the other kind—turned and walked back to where Fagin and Andrea waited. The officer playing the good guy left the room. The other motioned to them and they followed him outside into the hall of the building they were in. Staff Headquarters, Intelligence, Army of the Republic of South Vietnam.

"What do you think?" Fagin asked.

"He is a brave man," the captain said. "It will take a long time and much work to break him down."

Andrea was impatient. "He has information that we need as quickly as possible. There is no chance of

151

speeding up the process by beating him and giving him electric shocks. We already see that he has great resolve to resist that treatment. I think it is time for us to apply drugs."

"That is an application beyond our capabilities," the ARVN captain said.

"We have such facilities in Hai-Cat," Fagin said. "May I suggest he be transferred there?"

The captain was thoughtful for a few moments. Finally he nodded his head. "You are correct, of course. I shall begin the necessary paperwork."

Fagin looked back across the room where Gio, out of pride and pure guts, tried to stand straight under the merciless glare of the single bulb. "The trouble with this war," he said, "is that the other side has too many bastards like him!"

"He will break one way or the other," the captain said, not that impressed. "The drugs will be quicker, but only a completely insane man can resist a combination of physical and psychological torture over a long period of time."

"Time," Andrea said, "is something we do not have."

Archie Dobbs held his M16 over his head as he moved slowly and laboriously through the chest-deep water of the swamp. He carefully tested the soft, muddy bottom before each step. Any sudden fall on his part could cause a loud splash or send an unnatural ripple of water that might attract some alert NVA in the vicinity.

He had angled farther north than the usual route taken by the Goons during their patrols through the area. Archie did this to allow a "cushion of distance" to fall back on while moving around in the far reaches of the enemy's rear area. Soon the Black Eagle reached shallower water, continuing until he was out of the swamp and back onto the relatively dry terrain of the jungle.

Archie was stripped down even more than usual for

that particular mission. He had his ammo pouches clipped onto his cartridge belt along with two canteens. He carried his knife strapped around his right boot. The knife and the M16 rifle were all he had.

Lean and mean, Archie expected trouble.

Archie's amazing sense of orientation and direction, dormant during most of his life in the urban areas of Boston and Cambridge, Massachusetts, had been stoked to life through arduous Special Forces training and the combat experiences he'd gone through as a Black Eagle. Now that talent came to the fore as he moved westward in an unerring line that would take him to the exact spot he desired to be.

Archie had managed to reach a point so far behind the lines that he began to think he'd walked away from the war. At one point, because he thought perhaps the small bit of noise he made masked sounds of the enemy, the scout stopped and simply squatted down for a half hour. He waited and listened, every fiber of his being and senses finely tuned to the environment around him. But nothing disturbed the placid, heavy jungle.

Another half hour of cautious travel finally paid off. He came across a trail. The track, approximately six feet wide, had been worn in the jungle through constant use. Its discovery brought another period of watchful waiting, but at that time there seemed to be no activity.

Archie moved to the edge of the path and studied the footprints on it. He saw that they moved both up and down the trail. His expert eyes noted that those going toward the battle front were deeper in the ground than those coming back the other way. That offered but one conclusion: Heavily ladened supply details came from somewhere up the track, where a supply depot was located. The shallower footprints headed back were men returning for more material.

Anxious to see what sort of logistics setup served the front lines, Archie began slowly walking up toward the head of the trail. He carefully kept to one side so his G.I.

boots would leave no marks to alert the NVA of his presence.

Suddenly he heard talking men approaching.

He ducked back to cover, going low and waiting. Within a couple of minutes, a group of men carrying crates on litters appeared. As they trotted past he was able to get a good look at the cargo. The wooden boxes had two words that looked like MOPTNPA CHAPR stenciled on them. Archie recognized it as Russian. At one time Archie had seriously contemplated putting in for the language school at Monterey, California to study Russian. Falconi, whose mother was a native of the Soviet Union, helped him prepare by instructing him on how to read the Cyrillic alphabet.

Archie concentrated and tried to remember the letters of MOPTNPA CHAPR. He slowly mouthed to himself, "Mor-tee-rah snar-yah." He quickly realized the first word had to be Russian for mortar. The second, he guessed, probably meant shell. Meaning, of course, the supply details were busying themselves toting mortar shells up toward the battle front.

Archie moved farther up the trail until he noted it widening a bit. Going back into the cover of the jungle, he continued to travel along the track. Finally he reached the edge of a clearing. Neatly stacked within the clearing were a lot more crates marked MOPTNPA CHAPR. Archie settled down to mark the location on his map. As he worked, he was disturbed by the arrival of another group of men with litters. Quickly and wordlessly, they picked up some of the ammunition and returned in the direction of the trail. Then another litter team arrived. Then another. And another.

A determined effort to transport mortar rounds forward could only mean one thing: a big attack. Now Archie had to find the location of the actual battery that would fire the shells at the Black Eagles and their ARVN friends. He put the map back in his pocket and moved back, getting on the trail and carefully following the detail to whatever destination they sought.

Another group suddenly appeared from somewhere down the track. Archie quickly faded into the jungle to wait for them to pass. When they cleared the area, he went back to trailing the others. He had to hurry a bit to catch up with them. If he lost the litter team, it might take him a while to be able to find another as convenient.

Archie Dobbs certainly wasn't expecting to see the NVA officer who quite suddenly appeared in front of him.

Surprise lit up both men's eyes. The officer went for his holster. The one thing Archie couldn't afford was a shot to be fired. He leaped forward and tried a horizontal butt stroke with his rifle, but the nimble NVA ducked and came up with pistol drawn and ready to fire.

Archie dropped his M16 and grabbed the man's wrist, squeezing hard. He hoped to make the Red's hand go numb enough that he couldn't hang onto the weapon. Meanwhile he tried frantically to get his boot knife out, but the enraged NVA shook and pulled as he tried to free himself from the American's grip.

Snarling, the officer hissed, "Hang di!" He pushed hard, slowly bringing the muzzle closer to Archie's head.

Now the Black Eagle forgot the knife, using both hands to push back as he moved the pistol away from his face. Within moments he had it pointing straight at the officer's head while he kept squeezing in that wild hope to numb the man's hand.

The pistol went off.

The side of the NVA's head sprayed outward and his face collapsed inward. He immediately crumpled to the trail. Cursing silently, Archie bent down to pull the body off the trail. But shouts down the way and the sound of running feet showed that the supply detail was on the way to see what had happened.

Archie dove back to cover. He looked back and saw the officer sprawled there. For all intents and purposes it appeared as if he'd committed suicide. The pistol was still in his hand and from the way he lay, it was pointing at his temple. Archie started to congratulate himself, then he noticed that right beside the body, almost screaming it seemed, were his bootprints—as plain as if there was a sign pointing to them. For one desperate second Archie thought of rushing out to obliterate them, but it was too late.

The supply detail came into view making him pull back farther into the brush.

Chapter 16

The prisoner, dressed in a pair of nondescript U.S. Army unmarked fatigues, sat in the back of the staff car, displaying no signs of emotion. Burly South Vietnamese intelligence agents occupied the seats on both sides of him. The pair, expert in karate and the handling of captives, kept themselves on the alert for any resistance the POW might try.

Before leaving on the car trip, the captive's body cavities and even his teeth had been minutely examined to make sure no cyanide capsules or other life-taking drugs had been concealed on his person.

But Junior Sergeant Gio had no such devices.

Sophisticated and extravagant preparations were for highly trained, skilled operatives who worked in the clandestine world of spying. Gio was an infantryman—a combat veteran who slogged through the jungle—and his infiltration of American lines in the guise of a deserter had been simple, direct, and voluntary on his part. The noncommissioned officer was not a member of an elaborate spy organization, but he made up for his lack of finesse with fanatical dedication. But, though he was more than ready to die for his cause, he had no means to commit suicide.

They arrived at the gate of Hai-Cat and went through a thorough inspection by the military police guards there.

Even the ARVN officer in the front seat with the driver had to display his ID card and answer a few questions. He may have resented the intrusion on his privacy by soldiers of lesser rank, but he kept any displeasure he felt to himself. It was well known in the intelligence community that Hai-Cat and its regulations were to be taken seriously—damned seriously.

On the other hand, if Gio sensed he'd been brought to some important place he did not show it. The NVA soldier continued to stare icily out the windows, seemingly taking no notice of anything that came into his view. He even acted as if his attentive escorts were not there.

When the probe of the car and its passengers was completed, the American guard handed back their documents. "You'll find Mr. Fagin and Captain Thuy over in Building Six," he said. "You're expected." He looked at the prisoner. "You in particular, Bud."

Gio, though not understanding the words, sensed he'd been addressed. He looked at the American for a brief instant, then turned his eyes back to their aimless staring.

The ARVN chauffeur drove slowly through Hai-Cat, noting the numbers on the buildings. When he reached number six, the driver eased to a stop. The officer in the front immediately popped out of the car. He opened one of the back doors and the intelligence agent there stepped out, dragging Gio with him. The agent was quickly joined by his partner. Then, with the POW between them, they followed the officer into the building.

Gio vaguely wondered if he were being taken to a place of execution. He'd made up his mind that he would die on that last mission even before he'd crossed no-man's land and approached the MLR with his hands held high. He only hoped, deep in his heart, that he would be given a quick death by firing squad. During propaganda lectures, the political commissars had told the NVA soldiers that only painful, lingering deaths awaited them as prisoners of the Americans or South Vietnamese.

The NVA guards frog-marched him down a long hall to a door where a single American soldier stood. The G.I. checked IDs just as carefully as had his counterparts at the front gate. When he was satisfied all was in order, he opened the door and allowed them to enter. When they stepped inside the room, Gio finally showed some emotion.

He gasped.

The soldier could understand a beating—he'd given plenty in his day when his own side had prisoners. He had even killed POWs on orders from his superiors. That was no big thing for him. But the chamber seemed to be a hospital operating theatre of some sorts. A gurney with straps stood in the center of the room. Gio, remembering the commissars' warnings, could only regard the device as some sort of horrible instrument designed to inflict a hideous death on him. He also noted a strange-looking stand holding an upturned bottle with a long rubber tube running from it.

Whatever was about to happen was mysterious and alien to the simple man who had begun life as a rice farmer. He realized what he could see was part of something beyond his imagination, something that held only evil and doom for him. It scared the hell out of him.

Chuck Fagin stepped forward. "Strap him on."

Andrea Thuy waited for the NVA sergeant to be bound to the gurney. She took note of the wild look in his eyes and the perspiration that now flowed freely from his face. She had been a prisoner of the Reds on three occasions in her life. The young woman did nothing to hide the loathing and hatred she felt for the POW. Her voice was low and menacing as she spoke to him in Vietnamese:

"We are going to ask you some questions," Andrea said. "They are the same ones that were asked of you before."

Gio swallowed nervously but displayed a brave front. If he was going to die shrieking, he made up his mind he

159

would holler nothing but NVA patriotic and fighting slogans. "Chuc ba may man," he said with a sneer.

"I do not need good luck," Andrea said coldly. "You do." She grabbed his arm and squeezed, making the vein stand out. Then she inserted a needle into it. "You are going to talk, you bastard! You'll tell us everything we want to know. In fact, you will babble so much that within an hour we are going to wish you would shut up."

Puzzled and frightened, Gio looked up in her face. Within moments his vision grew misty, yet he felt good. This certainly didn't seem like it was going to be an unpleasant death. *Duoc roi!* As a matter of fact, he was beginning to experience sensations of peace and calm.

Then all consciousness slipped from his being and he drifted off into a world controlled by sodium pentothal. As he drifted under the influence of the drug, a stenographer came into the room carrying her own chair. A highly skilled taker of shorthand, she settled in to record minutely every question, answer, and comment of the session, which would prove to be long and laborious.

The NVA supply detail rushed up to the fallen officer. Archie sighed almost audibly as they scuffed up the bootprints he'd left on the trail as they gathered around the dead man. Within a few moments all the tracks he'd left behind were completely obliterated.

The Black Eagle quickly forgot his relief, however, and immediately concentrated on listening to the excited soldiers. Although not fluent in Vietnamese, he had an excellent working knowledge of the language and could understand it reasonably well. He was able to catch the meanings of phrases as the Red soldiers chattered in agitation among themselves:

"The comrade captain is dead. What has happened here?"

"Oh, look! He is shot—"

"See, comrades! His pistol is in his hand."

160

"Suicide! The comrade captain shot himself!"

"It has happened much, no? My comrade from my home village is in the third company. He said a lieutenant there killed himself with a grenade!"

"Yes! Morale is low in some of the companies!"

"Quiet, fool! You will be turned in as a defeatist!"

"Quick! We must report this!"

"No! Deliver the ammunition first. Then we report."

All the members of the supply detail agreed with the last speaker. After another moment of fussing around the cadaver, they rushed back to their litters of mortar ammo.

Archie grinned to himself. He always felt good when he got away with something. In a way, it was a sort of school-boy complex he had never outgrown. He was glad the supply detail would deliver the mortar shells. He could track them to the spot where the heavy weapons were located. That was one of the chores Falconi had assigned him.

The soldiers left the officer and hurried back to their litters, pausing only long enough to heave the heavy burdens up on their shoulders before resuming their trek down the trail.

Archie, moving as fast as the need for silence and the thickness of the brush permitted, followed.

In only fifteen minutes they reached their destination. It looked familiar to the Black Eagle—as well it should. It was the same location where the damned recoilless rifle had pumped shell after shell into the hiding place of the parachute infiltrators. It wasn't far from the original mortar battery where Colonel Falconi had been so generous with his supply of thermite grenades. In fact, the ruined tubes could easily be seen stacked a few meters off the trail.

The burning question still remained. Where had the replacement weapons come from? The thorough scouting done by the Goons had noted every supply cache in the NVA rear area. Not a single one had contained extra mortars.

Archie's eyes widened as another thought occurred to him.

He had seen the supply dump where these mortar rounds had come from. He recalled there had been rations and small-arms ammo there before. That meant the mortar shells had been brought there recently from some other place.

But where?

Archie grinned and said to himself, "Pal, that's exactly what the colonel wants you to find out. Now get humping!" He pulled back into the brush and retraced his steps up the trail. When he reached the dead officer he noted that the cadaver was already covered with ants. Dead bodies did not last long in the tropics, with its hot environment and hungry scavengers. Archie shuddered and winced, quickly moving past the awful sight.

When Archie reached the supply dump, he carefully worked his way around to the opposite side. He had spotted another trail leading there. That could only be the link between the military goods stored in the area and the place which from they had been laboriously toted. Archie finally found a good spot in a grove of leather fern.

He settled down to wait.

Chuck Fagin and Andrea Thuy walked slowly from Building Six and headed for their office on the other side of Hai-Cat. Back in the interrogation room, Junior Sergeant Gio had already awakened from his drug-induced sleep. Groggy and uncomprehending, he had been dragged roughly from the gurney and walked around by his guard to get him wide awake.

"Is there any chance for the drug to fail?" Fagin asked.

"Not in this case," Andrea said. "Although the prisoner is highly motivated and politically indoctrinated to the point of fanaticism, he isn't sophisticated enough

162

to fully realize what has happened to him."

"There have to be some clues in what he said," Fagin mused. "The man might be ignorant of what went on around him, but something must have registered in his subconscious mind that his conscious mind gave no thought to."

"We won't know until we study the transcript of what he said," Andrea told him.

"While we're waiting for the steno to type it up, let's have a good stiff belt," Fagin suggested. He grinned. "Irish whiskey, of course!"

"A great idea!" Andrea exclaimed. She had worn herself out in the long questioning of the NVA prisoner.

It had been extremely difficult to get Gio to concentrate for any length of time. Any direct question would get a quick, simple answer. Further attempts to get him to elaborate would soon have him babbling about a multitude of subjects. Fagin's rough notes showed that for the first hour, the NVA sergeant discussed:

—the various supply dumps in the operational area

—a particular trail that led from the dumps to the main line of resistance

—his first piece of ass at age thirteen

—the number of men in his rifle section

—a chickenshit lieutenant over in another company

—and a Chinese movie he had particularly liked during his last trip to Hanoi

"Do you realize how much shit we've got to wade through?" Fagin asked Andrea when they arrived at their office. He held the door open for her.

"I can't understand you being so surprised," Andrea said, preceding him into the building. "Actually, I expected this. It's all quite normal in such an interrogation. Don't worry about it."

"Well, you've had special training in that sort of interrogation back at Langley," Fagin conceded. "I was

163

given the short course: how to use a rubber hose."

"How crude!" Andrea said with a good-humored wink. "Now shut up and bring out that bottle."

Fagin went to the wet bar and pulled out a couple of glasses. He got some ice cubes from the small fridge underneath it, putting the rocks in one glass. "I don't like foreign objects in my Irish whiskey," he explained.

"Particularly if it dilutes it, right?" Andrea asked.

"Right!" Fagin poured the drink. There was a rustle at the door and he looked up.

Donegan, Choy, and McKeever appeared in the office. "Hey!" the pilot hollered. "Do you have any Guinness Stout?"

"Jesus Christ!" Fagin said. "I knew if I went to the bar you three would show up."

"You didn't answer his question at you," McKeever said in his inimical style. "Does you got'ny Guinness Stout?"

"Yes, as a matter of fact, I *does,*" Fagin said. He walked around the bar. "Help yourselves. It's been a long day and I need to sit down and relax."

McKeever fetched three bottles of the brew and passed them to his friends. The three airmen made themselves comfortable on the sofa. McKeever downed three-quarters of his bottle and belched.

"God!" Andrea complained.

"Well, at least I din't fart," McKeever said defending himself. "I got good manners."

"Knock it off," Donegan said. He looked at Fagin. "How'd it go?"

"It looks a big zero," Fagin explained. "But we're going to peruse the transcript of the proceedings when they get over here with 'em. Andrea thinks we can find some clues in there somewhere."

"You better," Choy said seriously. "Falconi and his boys work in the dark out there. He need much information. You betcha!"

"They should pack it in," Donegan said seriously.

"The situation is strictly no-win. Why does he insist on sticking it out?"

"You know Falconi," Fagin said. "He's never quit on anything in his life."

"Can I have another of 'em Guinesses?" McKeever asked.

"Hell, no!"

"T'ank you kindly," McKeever said getting up to fetch himself one. He went back to the sofa and sat down.

Fagin sighed. "Oh, well."

Andrea sipped her drink. "You sound worried, Donegan. Do you want to pack it in?"

"You know better'n that, Andrea," Donegan said. "As long as Falconi and the Black Eagles need air support, we'll be there through hell or high water."

"Can I have another of 'em Guinesses?" McKeever asked.

"Damn! Did you already finish that one?" Fagin complained. "Get two or three at a time. And stop asking if it's all right."

"Okay."

Donegan ignored the banter. "I want to say one thing. If you don't dig some sort of intelligence out of what that damned NVA pris'ner said, then we can kiss our ol' buddy Falconi goodbye. Because he'll stay out there 'til him and that whole Black Eagle bunch of his gets croaked!"

"You betcha!" Choy said.

Chapter 17

Archie had allowed himself some intermittent napping because of inactivity in the supply dump. These bouts of dozing lasted no longer than five to ten minutes at a time, since even the slight buzz of an occasional flying insect woke him up. Being far behind enemy lines and hiding in their midst does not encourage a relaxing attitude in anyone—even Archie Dobbs.

A single guard watched the place, which indicated to the Black Eagle that the NVA considered the area as secure as could be expected. That made Archie grin. He wondered what the enemy commander would think if he knew an infiltrator was casually observing the goings-on in the far rear of his unit area.

The day dragged slowly into evening. The routine was broken when the guard was relieved by another soldier. The new sentry, an efficient sort, began his tour of duty with a quick inspection of the place by walking the entire perimeter. The NVA came so close to Archie's hiding place that the interloper was forced to duck down, drawing his knife in case of discovery. But the NVA failed to see him and went back to his post.

When darkness finally settled over the scene, Archie decided to get some real sleep. At least, as close as he could get to sleep. The Black Eagle knew that he would not be able to slumber soundly through the entire night.

His adrenalin was pumping away from being in the midst of people who would gladly drag him out and summarily execute him if they found him. Either that or he would be shipped off to a long period of confinement as a prisoner of war. It was well known that men had been held in unspeakable conditions for years by the Reds.

Such concerns do not contribute to a man's ability to relax.

But the infiltrator could at least get in a comfortable position. That way he could enjoy some rather deep dozing, dozing that at times might last as long as fifteen or twenty minutes before an awareness of where he was and what he was doing popped through his subconscious mind and woke him up.

Archie moved cautiously, looking as if he were in a movie scene shot in slow-motion as he sat back on his butt. Taking a deep breath, he eased back to rest against one of the plants in the grove of leather fern that concealed him. After laying his M16 across his lap for easy access, the Black Eagle finally allowed himself to relax. He closed his eyes and drifted off to sleep.

The first period of napping was light and shallow, lasting no more than five minutes. Then his eyes popped open and he carefully sat up, looking out into the clearing that contained the supply dump. It was pitch black, and he could see neither the goods stored there nor the sentry.

Archie leaned back and closed his eyes again.

This time he drifted deeper into the arms of Morpheus. He actually dreamed. His dozing mind conjured up his ex-girlfriend, Betty Lou Pemberton, the one who had dumped him. She was in her nurse uniform giving out donuts and hot coffee to a group of G.I.s standing in a line. Archie joined the queue and waited as he worked his way up to her. But each time it became his turn to be served, Betty Lou would scowl at him and order him to the rear.

"Bitch!" Archie said aloud.

Cursing himself for talking in his sleep, he immediately came awake, holding his M16 rifle. Expecting the absolute worst, Archie peered through the inky blackness around him and listened nervously for some sort of sound from the sentry. When none came, he relaxed.

The dream had awakened old feelings, and he became good and mad at Betty Lou. A few months before she had given him an ultimatum—leave the Black Eagles or she would leave him. It had broken his heart, but he stayed true to Colonel Falconi and the rest of the guys. Now, with the demanding young woman very much on his mind, he was so pissed off he couldn't get back to sleep. Gritting his teeth, he scowled in the darkness, staring out into the tropical night.

Then Archie saw the red light blink—once, twice, three times.

He knew what it was because he also used such a device on various occasions in his military career. It was a regular flashlight with a red filter attached to it. These were used at night to keep down the glare when making necessary signals in the darkness. Also, the redness of the glow didn't affect night vision.

He looked over at the other side of the unseen supply dump and saw another light blink three times. Evidently it was a recognition signal of sorts. The first light, held by the sentry, moved across the area to the second. Archie could hear some low muttering followed by the sound of numerous people walking. Some clunks and scratching noises puzzled Archie at first. Then he realized that a nocturnal delivery of supplies was being made as he sat there. He pulled his knife from the boot scabbard and stuck it in the ground, leaning it in the direction of the second light. When morning came, the handle would point directly at the spot the supplies had come in from.

Then he would have located the hidden logistics trail.

Andrea poured over the transcript of the interrogation

of the NVA noncommissioned officer. The testimony was one hundred and thirteen pages long, typewritten, double-spaced in romanized Vietnamese script. Chuck Fagin, Tim Donegan, Mike McKeever, and Choy lounged around the room as she read intermittently from the document.

Actually, McKeever was paying no attention. He lay on the floor beside the sofa, snoozing away with his belly filled with Guinness Stout.

The written record had been made in Vietnamese by a native stenographer employed by the ARVN's intelligence service. Andrea not only had to read it aloud, she had to translate it into English for the benefit of the others in the room.

"Read the part about the joy girls again," Tim asked her. He referred to the statements made by Junior Sergeant Gio in reference to the prostitutes furnished by the NVA for the soldiers' enjoyment during rest periods away from the fighting.

Fagin snorted. "You just want to hear the dirty stuff."

"Oh, hell no!" Donegan protested. "I'm planning on pursuing studies in Asian cultures when I leave the agency. This information will be very handy when I submit my thesis for a Ph.D."

"I didn't know they gave Ph.D.s in bullshit," Fagin said. He laughed. "Timothy Donegan, Ph.D., B.S."

Andrea wasn't amused. "Shut up! There is some important information here and we must ferret it out."

"Why didn't you just ask him what you wanted?" Choy inquired. "Much easier, no?"

"That is not possible under the drug," Andrea explained. "All one can do is ask, then the subject begins talking about the subject brought up. It is a lot like remembering things. One incident reminds him of another and another and another. He told us what we wanted to know, but only in a disjointed, confusing sequence. Like I said, it's all in there someplace. But we must pull it out and make it understandable."

"Okay then," Fagin said. "I have an idea." He walked over to Andrea and handed her a black felt pen from his pocket. "Why don't you mark out everything we know doesn't pertain to the situation out there between Tay Ninh and An Loc? That way we won't have to deal with the useless crap he babbled at us."

"Good idea," Andrea said. She turned back to page one and began reading again. "Obviously, his school days in his native village don't pertain much to the SITREP." She used the pen to mark out that section of the transcript.

"Leave the joy-girl stuff in," Tim said.

"Shut up, Donegan," Andrea said calmly as she continued her careful perusal. The pen scratched a few more times as she went through the pages.

"This will take a bit of time," Fagin said. He went to his bar and poured a tumbler of Irish whiskey.

"Any stout left?" Donegan asked.

"Hell no!" Fagin barked. He pointed to the sleeping McKeever. "Shithead there drank it all."

"Wait a minute!" Andrea called out. "Here's something that's interesting. I don't think we've paid much attention to it before."

Fagin went back and sat down. "Let's hear it."

Andrea read, "Rice paddies torn up . . . Major Hyun's orders . . . bamboo planted . . . peasants run off . . . Captain Ngoi hit old man . . . too bad rice gone . . . caves to dig . . . caves to cover."

Fagin took a sip of his drink. "That probably doesn't mean anything. Gio is probably remembering something that happened in his home village."

"No," Andrea said. "Don't forget that he named a Major Hyun as his battalion commander and Captain Gio as the deputy. When those peasants were run off, it had to be in the operational area."

"So they evacuated some peasants," Donegan said. "That's not unusual."

"Sure," Choy chimed in. "Our side do it too, remember? They go to protective hamlets."

"There are no protective hamlets out there where the Black Eagles are fighting that NVA battalion," Andrea said. "And it is too far south for the Reds to transport peasants up to North Vietnam." She shook her head. "Something else went down out there and it has to do with the current mission."

"So we're talking about tearing up rice paddies and moving peasants," Fagin said. "That was more than likely done to rid the area of any potential threats."

"What about planting bamboo?" Andrea asked. "What do you make of that?"

"That does bother me," Fagin admitted. "Why in the hell would an NVA unit deep in the South and facing constant combat go to the trouble of cultivating bamboo? Especially when there must be plenty of the stuff around anyhow?"

"No sense! No sense!" Choy exclaimed. "Bamboo is crazy stuff. Grow fast and strong. Can never get rid of it."

"From what Gio said it sounds like they planted it in old rice paddies or something," Andrea said, rereading that particular part.

"Oh, Jesus!" Fagin exclaimed. "I think Gio was a babbling idiot! The idea of substituting bamboo for rice is so crazy it isn't worth considering."

"We're wasting our time," Donegan said. He glanced through the window. "Look, the sun is coming up."

"A new day," Fagin said. "I say we knock it off and call this a lost cause. Anybody want to go over to the dining hall with me for breakfast?"

McKeever instantly sat up. "Somebody say breakfast?"

"Yeah, you big bastard," Fagin growled. "C'mon. We're gonna eat."

"Go ahead," Andrea said. "I'm going through this thing one more time. Then I'll pull some statements out and radio them to Falconi in the field. Maybe out there where all this stuff happened, he can make some sense

171

out of this intelligence—if that's what it is."

"Good luck," Fagin said. "C'mon, guys. I hear a plate of ham and eggs calling to me."

Archie Dobbs stirred in his hiding spot for about the twentieth time. But this time, instead of going back to sleep, he came wide awake. The sun was already high enough to lighten the area and he could dimly see the sentry standing at his post. The Black Eagle remembered the supply detail that had shown up flashing red signals. He looked down at his knife and noted which direction the handle was pointing. It showed him the exact point where the NVA lugging the supplies had entered the clearing. He took another look at the clearing and could see the crates that had been brought in by the nocturnal workers. The goods were stacked neatly off to one side.

Archie sheathed the knife and slowly stood up. He moved carefully through the leather ferns, making sure he stepped on nothing that would make noise. He continued in this laborious fashion for a full hour before he managed to reach the spot where the litter bearers had shown up. A search of the ground showed some footprints in the dirt. Archie traced them back toward the direction they seemed to come from.

Then he found the trail.

It was cut through high bamboo. The American, much taller than the short Vietnamese who used the track, had to bend over as he followed it northward. He noted how unusual the growth of the bamboo was. He appeared to be in a virtual forest of the stuff. Generally, in the tropical jungles of the area, all sorts of vegetation shared the terrain.

He climbed several narrow ridges, which were approximately six feet high and perhaps a yard across at the top. Each one, set at a regular interval with the other, seemed to be a divider of some sort. Because of that evenness of spacing, he quickly surmised they were man-made.

But why would anyone have gone into the jungle and constructed such a weird earthen structure? The ridges were too far apart to make a good infantry defensive position. The flat areas between the ridges were the wrong size for mortar or artillery sites. They were useless even as tank traps.

Archie continued his reconnaissance until he had passed completely through the bamboo forest and had reentered the jungle. There was nothing else to find. Aside from marking down the relocations of a few old places and putting in some new ones, his entire mission was a bust.

Archie, disgusted, wiped at the sweat on his brow. It was time to get back to his own lines and give Falconi what little intelligence he had garnered.

Everything—the mission, the attacks, the entire operation, the parachute infiltration—added up to one big zip.

"SNAFU," Archie growled to himself. "Situation Normal, All Fucked Up."

Chapter 18

The radio transmission from Hai-Cat was of much importance and demanded absolute accuracy in receipt. Although the message was originally spoken in Vietnamese, it had been accurately translated by Andrea Thuy before being broadcast in English. For those reasons, Colonel Robert Falconi had his deputy commander, Captain Ray Swift Elk, take it down in its five-character word groups rather than have the usual Vietnamese ranger radio operator receive the transmission.

The Sioux officer dutifully recorded each dit and dah. As a former Special Forces intelligence sergeant, he had been cross-trained in communications. His expertise in that particular skill was right up to snuff and then some. The standards in the Green Berets were considerably higher than those in other units, which meant that a cross-trained Special Forces man was much higher qualified than someone in another unit, even though the skill involved was that man's primary military occupational specialty.

"Goddamn it!" Swift Elk exclaimed when the transmission was completed and decoded.

"What's the matter, Ray?" Falconi asked.

"This message doesn't make sense," Swift Elk said. "It's from Andrea. I recognize her fist." Each radio operator had distinct style or "fist" when tapping out code. It was as recognizable to another commo man as a voice. "Supposedly she's sending us some information they got from that phony deserter who came waltzing into our lines some time ago."

Falconi laughed. "Oh, yeah! The famous Junior Sergeant Gio. I'll bet the South Vietnamese intel boys put him through the proverbial mill."

"It wasn't the South Vietnamese who broke him. The prisoner was taken to Hai-Cat and juiced for interrogation," Swift Elk explained. "But it seems to me they didn't get shit out of him." He handed the paper over to Falconi. "Read it."

"Sure," Falconi said. The colonel took the missive and quickly skimmed over the call signs and opening statement. He read:

> Rice paddies torn up . . . Major Hyun's orders . . . bamboo planted . . . peasants run off . . . Captain Ngoi hit old man . . . too bad rice gone . . . caves to dig . . . caves to cover . . .

Falconi shrugged. "I can't make sense of it." He passed the message over to the ARVN commander, Colonel Long Kuyen, who sat beside him. "What do you think of this, Colonel?"

Kuyen read. "This is from the prisoner under interrogation? It is disjointed."

"He was under drugs," Swift Elk explained. "Andrea said it was sodium pentothal."

"Ah!" Kuyen said. "Now I understand." He read it again. "I presume this was spoken in Vietnamese."

"Undoubtedly," Falconi said. "As I recall, the prisoner was unable to speak English."

"Perhaps something is lost in translation," Kuyen suggested. "It would be better if they sent us the statement as the prisoner actually uttered it."

"Good idea," Falconi said. "Swift Elk, I'm going to have my regular radioman send the request. We'll

175

maintain a purity of language that way."

"Good idea, sir," Swift Elk said.

Falconi motioned to the Vietnamese radio operator. "Toi muon phien ong. Please operate the radio for the next transmission in your own language."

The ARVN soldier complied. At the end of the second broadcast he handed it over to his commander. Colonel Kuyen now read it in Vietnamese. He sighed. "It says the same thing. Such simple statements mean nothing to me."

"What's that Shakespeare said?" Falconi remarked. "Told by an idiot, full of sound and fury, signifying nothing."

"I don't know, sir," Ray Swift Elk said disagreeing. "I don't think a guy under sodium pentothal would be full of sound and fury. What he said is important. We just got to figure it out."

"You know," Falconi said irritably. "I've never been real enthused about puzzles, riddles, and word games. To tell you the truth, I really hate shit like this."

"Just keep in mind that the prisoner didn't purposely try to confuse anybody," Swift Elk reminded him. "What he gave us were disjointed, disorganized statements about things that really happened. He's speaking out of context."

"Then put the goddamned thing back into context if you're so fucking smart," Falconi said irritably. "Jesus Christ! Once an intelligence sergeant, always an intelligence sergeant."

"That Eleven-Foxtrot MOS means brains," Swift Elk said confidently. "We're the cream of the noncommissioned officer class."

"You mean *they're* the cream," Falconi reminded him. "You're a captain now."

"But, sir," Swift Elk said grinning. "You just said that once—"

"At ease!" Falconi interrupted growling. "And get to work!" He softened a bit and smiled back. "You son of a bitch. I'll bet you're as proud of your operations-intelligence background as you are of your commission, aren't you?"

Swift Elk, enjoying the chance to goad his commander, started to reply when someone approaching caught his attention. "Look what the cat dragged in," Ray said pointing.

Falconi and Kuyen turned to see Archie Dobbs, bedraggled and soaked in sweat and swamp water, approaching them in a slow, tired gait.

He walked up to Falconi and rendered a salute. "Well, sir, I'm back. I just wish I could say mission accomplished. But sorry. I did my best."

"Okay, Archie," Falconi said. "Let's pull up some ground here and sit down. Just give me your report."

Archie settled down in the dirt beside the detachment commander. The Black Eagle scout pulled his map from his side trouser pocket. "I've got some coordinates that should come in handy, sir." He spread the chart out. "Here's the new mortar position."

Falconi looked at the mark. "That's where we were pinned down by the recoilless rifle."

"Yes, sir," Archie said. "The NVA bastards hauled the bodies away and moved in their mortars. By the way, the ones you spoiled with them thermite grenades are stacked off the trail there."

"What else did you find, Archie?" Falconi asked.

"A few more supply dumps," Archie answered. "There, there, there, and there. And there." He put his finger down on each mark. "Some of 'em are ones us Goons found earlier. Others are new."

"It looks to me like you've done a damn good job," Falconi said.

"Thank you, sir," Archie said. "But I didn't find where them new mortars came from. I looked around and thought I was on to something, but I hit a dead end. By then I was out of time and had to come back. I'm real sorry, Colonel. I done my best, honest."

177

"I'm sure you did," Falconi said. He shook his head. "I wish we could have found that main supply cache, though. If we nailed it, then we could move in there and wipe that NVA completely off the face of the earth."

Swift Elk spoke up. "But as long as they can bring up new mortars and other heavy weaponry, we'll just sit here and slam against the bastards until both sides are wiped out."

"That's a kind of victory, ain't it?" Archie asked.

"Not my kind," Falconi said. "I don't consider getting my command wiped out to massacre the bad guys a good trade-off."

"Me neither, sir," Archie said. He smiled. "Particularly when I'm one of the jokers getting wiped out."

Falconi checked the map again. "I guess the best we can do is hit these supply dumps and the new mortar battery then charge in and hope we've kicked their asses quicker than they can resupply their line units."

Archie shook his head. "I don't think we can pull it off, sir. The NVA logistical situation is well organized. They can run stuff anyplace they want real fast."

"Shit!" Falconi said. He found the no-win situation maddening. "Is there anything else you saw back there?"

"Yes, sir," Archie said. "But it's not worth much. I stayed the night watching one resupply dump there—" He showed the exact spot on the map. "—and saw a night delivery of mortar rounds. I found the trail they came in on, but it led to an immense bamboo grove." He shook his head. "The strange thing about it is that it looked like the bamboo had been planted over some old rice paddies. The ridges between the paddies was still there."

"What!" Falconi exclaimed.

"Jesus Christ!" Swift Elk yelled. "Go on, Archie!"

"What the hell's the matter with you two?" Archie asked. "I only said I found bamboo growing over some old rice paddies."

Falconi leaned forward. "And there was a resupply trail through the place?"

178

"Yes, sir," Archie replied puzzled.

Swift Elk got the message and read it aloud. "It's all here, Colonel Falconi! Listen! 'Rice paddies torn up, bamboo planted—'"

"Right!" Falconi exclaimed. "They ran the peasants off, took their rice paddies and covered them with bamboo. That's the fastest growing stuff they could find."

"But why do that?" Archie asked.

Swift Elk ignored him and continued with the message. "Then it said 'Caves to dig, caves to cover.' Ha! Where's the best place to hide something?"

"In the open," Falconi answered. Then he added. "Then cover it with bamboo."

"What message? What are you talking about?" Archie wanted to know.

"The NVA ran the peasants out of the area, then dug supply caves in the rice paddies," Falconi explained. "They planted bamboo that quickly covered the place. While everyone looked in the jungle for supply caches the stuff was stashed under that innocent-looking bamboo in an area that most maps showed as rice paddies anyhow."

Archie was still in the dark. "What goddamned message are you talking about?"

"Did you mark that bamboo on your map?" Falconi asked.

"Yes, sir. It's right there, see? Now will anyone answer my question?"

"Give me the radio," Falconi said. "I've got some new targets for Donegan and his crew to hit. Then we're going to plow into that goddamned NVA line and *really* kick butt."

Archie stood up and howled, "Will somebody please tell me what the fuck is going on?"

Chapter 19

The orderly rapped lightly on the top of the hootch. "Mot tach che, Thieu-ta," he announced.

Major Tanh Hyun, commander of the NVA battalion, awoke. He had gone to bed the night before fully dressed as he always did. All he had to do was reach over and grab his web gear and AK47 before rolling out of the palm-covered shelter to accept the hot cup of tea from the soldier who served as his orderly and cook.

"Chao ong," the major said politely to the man.

"Chao ong, Thieu-ta," came the proper reply.

The orderly was an old soldier who had been seriously wounded two years before. He walked with a pronounced limp and was virtually useless as a front-line infantryman anymore. But he had spent so much time in war—first against the Japanese, then the French, and finally the South Vietnamese and the Americans—that he could never hope to adapt to a peaceful lifestyle and retire to his home village or even the old soldiers home in Hanoi. The orderly stayed with an active unit by choice, happy to share the dangers and hardships with his commanding officer.

After serving the officer, the orderly returned to the cookfire to continue his chores.

Major Hyun sipped the hot brew and looked around in the dim predawn light.

Some front-line troops detailed as ration carriers were already appearing from the MLR to pick up their unit's issue of rice and tea. When they had first arrived in the area, they'd eaten relatively well, not only from their own supplies but from the stores of overrun ARVN ranger units. There had been veritable feasts that ended with full bellies, contented belching, and happy laughter. But such loot garnered from the victories they'd enjoyed in the past were gone. Since the Americans had arrived on the scene to direct the South Vietnamese, the situation had bogged down to stubborn fighting on the line, with nothing gained by either side. Because of that, Major Hyun's soldiers now received one issue of rice and tea per day. They had to supplement the diet with wild jungle fruit and vegetables. But now, with most of the trees ruined, that was impossible. The lush rain forest had been reduced to tangled piles of blasted trees and brush, the natural bounty of food all but completely destroyed.

Hyun knew that as long as the situation continued he would eventually lose this campaign. But he could make his enemies pay dearly for the victory. His unit strengths had dwindled considerably, but his supply caches guaranteed that they could last quite a bit longer, then make one desperate last stand, a stand that would end in defeat but that would inflict heavy casualties on the enemy as well. There was an even chance that the attackers would lose more men than he would.

The orderly reappeared with a half bowl of rice. Hyun, who ate the same kind of food and in a like amount as his men, took the meal and consumed it slowly, saving the last of his tea to wash it down. He thought about the late Captain Ngoi, who had died during the final breakout of the parachute infiltrators. Ngoi had been a good officer, paying attention to all the details necessary in running the sort of unstable operation they faced there in the South. Although a nervous sort, he could be counted on to perform his duties above average. Hyun missed his

181

services and support.

Forgetting his troubles, the NVA major smiled to himself. It was obvious the infiltrators had risked their necks to come in and destroy his mortars. They must have been happy as they dropped the thermite grenades down the tubes and saw the heavy weaponry melt. Yet the attackers were almost wiped out by that recoilless rifle crew until their desperate bid for escape. Hyun had to admire the leader of those raiders, whoever he was, for the man literally led his men out of the jaws of death. By all accounts they should have been blown to bloody hunks of meat by the 57-millimeter shells.

Now Hyun laughed aloud. But the sons of a bitches must have been shocked when they launched their attack later and charged straight into a most unexpected mortar barrage.

The major's thoughts were suddenly interrupted by the sound of the approaching plane.

The engine noise was easily identifiable as the flying devil that had strafed and bombed them before. The crew of the aircraft was able to hit targets with amazing accuracy. But Hyun was not worried at this point. He had placed the new mortars in a different location from the others and shifted several of the more important supply depots.

Within moments the low-flying airplane swept over with machine guns blasting. All the NVA recognized the unusual shape of the Catalina's fuselage as its heavy slugs slammed into the ground and the vegetation in swarms, kicking up dirt and twigs. Everyone in the vicinity, including Hyun, dove to cover as the metal storm roared around them. A few unfortunates were caught in the open, their lives blasted from the body by the .50-caliber slugs.

Then the bombs went off.

Hyun could not tell exactly where they had hit. The ground shook with the force of the explosions. The heavy smell of spent explosive could be detected, and oily, black

182

smoke rose into the sky.

Within moments another stick of the explosives slammed into the earth farther away.

This was immediately followed by an additional, louder, and more violent series of detonations that created a small earthquake. Hyun knew where those bombs had fallen—right on his hidden ammunition and weapon caches in the caves under the bamboo.

Was it a lucky hit or did the devils know what they were after?

Now more trouble popped up in the major's agitated environment. Firing up on the MLR broke out, then built up in a flow but sure crescendo until there was no doubt that a full-scale attack had been launched against the NVA positions.

A lone soldier appeared from the front. He was badly wounded and he staggered in pain. His tunic was so soaked in blood that a red trickle dribbled from one sleeve.

"Comrade Major!" he cried in anguish. "The mortars are gone!"

"Gone? Gone?" Hyun bellowed.

"Yes, Comrade Major. Bombs fell directly on our position," the injured soldier reported. "I am the only survivor."

"How did they find you? Were you not properly camouflaged?" Hyun shrieked.

"Yes, Comrade Major—" The man sank to his knees, the severe loss of blood draining his strength away. "Comrade Major, our camouflage was . . . perfect . . . but the bombs . . . hit us with uncanny accuracy—"

Hyun clenched his fists in rage. "The bastards! The bastards! They knew where we had placed the new mortars. They had the exact location!"

The wounded man had more bad news. "We cannot . . . we cannot replace them, Comrade Major . . . the supply caves under the bamboo have—"

"Curse their mothers! Curse their ancestors!" Hyun

screamed. He now knew the explosions following the bombing were his entire ammo and weapon resupply going up.

Now runners appeared from the Main Line of Resistance. They all had the same report: "The entire South Vietnamese unit has launched an attack along the line! Orders, Comrade Major?"

And Major Tanh Hyun had the same order for all of them:

"Fight to the death!"

Chapter 20

Sergeant Major Top Gordon's Second Assault Commando, occupying the center of the line, moved forward into the enemy positions. The ARVN rangers hit the NVA with M16 rifles, M203 grenade launchers, and M60 machine guns blazing. The amount of tracer fire ripping from their attack formation looked like a mass of fiery streaks.

Top, his second-in-command, Sergeant Steve Matsuno, and their South Vietnamese troops appeared as demons straight out of hell to the NVA infantrymen across the battle front.

The rounds slammed and slapped into the enemy MLR. The Red unit commanders vainly called for mortar fire to break up the storm of troops coming at them, but their runners would find nothing in the rear areas. The bombs from Donegan's PBY had reduced the heavy weapons unit to a pile of bloody sludge and smashed tubes.

The only heavy weaponry in the entire battle came from Chief Warrant Officer Calvin Culpepper's battery.

Firing a carefully conceived and plotted barrage, the Black Eagle's mortarmen pumped round after round of 81-millimeter shells into their tubes. The projectiles blasted out to fall accurately between the enemy's main and second lines of resistance. The fusillade was pinpointed to such a degree that it cut the NVA forces in two, separating them with blasting explosions of shrapnel and concussion.

Captain Ray Swift Elk had completely recovered from his ordeal of sleeplessness as commander during Colonel Robert Falconi's parachute infiltration mission. Fresh, eager, and filled with Sioux battle ardor, he led the men of his First Assault Commando straight into the right side of the enemy's line.

The NVA resisted bitterly, throwing out volleys of rifle and machine gun fire, making the First's attack bog down a bit. But Paulo Garcia, commanding a special raiding force, took his troops on a wide end-run, then turned abruptly. Without taking the time to set up support fire, relying on shock alone, the marine staff sergeant bowled into the Red's flank. He caught them unaware, slaughtering their soldiers in that area of the battle front.

When, because of Paulo's efforts, the pressure lessened, Swift Elk leaped up and led an all-out assault that swept over the demoralized NVA. At that point of the combat, the battle turned from fighting to slaughter, until the more prudent of the enemy began throwing down their weapons and surrendering. The First Commando ended up with so many prisoners they had to detail some men to take them to the rear.

Meanwhile, Master Sergeant Malpractice McCorckel was not letting his Third Assault Commando take it easy. Formed in three waves, they scrambled across the downed trees and brush, diving into the enemy positions with bayonets and rifle butts. Vicious hand-to-hand fighting raged in that sector until Sergeant Gunnar Olson, performing his own out-flanking maneuver, crashed into the NVA and shattered their fighting positions. The Reds' resistance crumbled as they either surrendered or died.

But the middle of the battle still raged hot and heavy, without any sign of let-up.

Colonel Robert Falconi, personally leading the Goons, took his group up to the front and joined Top Gordon's first line assault troops. For a bit they moved in with the front line, blending in with the rifle squads there. Rifle volleys blasted out from both sides, with Top's machine gun crews sweeping support fire over their heads, the waving, sliding salvos peppering the enemy defensive line.

After a full fifteen minutes of the heavy shooting, Falconi judged the time was right. He grabbed the handset of his radio and raised Warrant Officer Calvin Culpepper:

"Checkmate Four, this is Checkmate!" Falconi broadcasted. "Lift your fire! I say again! Lift your fire! Out!"

In less than five seconds the mortar barrage ended and the final shells fell from the sky and crashed down on the battlefront. That was Falconi's signal to make the final move he had been striving for since the bloody operation had begun.

"All Checkmates! As skirmishers!" he ordered. "All right, you grubby bastards! Forward!"

That last attack began at a slow walk, then built up into a trot for another fifteen meters. Sweeping sprays of M16 and M60 fire crumbled the last bits of resistance on the NVA Main Line of Resistance.

Now Falconi, ahead of everyone else, broke into an all-out run. With Loco Padilla, Archie Dobbs, Blue Richards, Ky Luyen, and ARVN Corporal Trang Ngo behind him, the colonel led the smash into the Second Line of Resistance.

He leaped across a fallen log and threw a vicious horizontal butt stroke against an NVA. The butt of the rifle struck the Red soldier so hard it spun the man around 360 degrees before he toppled unconscious to the ground.

Blue Richards took out the final desperate efforts of a Red machine gun crew with a deadly, splattering round of buckshot from his M203.

Archie Dobbs dropped to his knee to aim four quick shots that took out as many NVA, while Ky Luyen and

Trang Ngo tossed grenades that blew away the final charge of three fanatical enemy soldiers.

Top, Steve, and the rangers now caught up and swept forward to put the final *coup de grâce* on resistance. A brief flurry of firing built up then quickly died off. A ringing, deafening silence engulfed the scene.

The campaign was over.

It was Archie Dobbs who found the dead NVA commander. He was easily recognized by the epaulets on his field shirt. He'd been hit several times, the distorted expression on his face showing the violence of his death. Nearby, an old soldier lay where he'd fallen beside his commander.

The man who had killed him, Sergeant Steve Matsuno, had noted the NVA had limped badly while attacking him. An examination of the cadaver showed the cause of the infirmity was not a fresh wound but an old one.

"The ancient bastard should've taken a medical pension and retired," Steve remarked.

Colonel Robert Falconi was satisfied. He smiled grimly as the other assault commandos moved into the area to search out any enemy survivors and either take them prisoner or treat their wounds.

Sergeant Major Top Gordon slung his rifle over his shoulder. "Chalk this one up as a victory, sir."

Ray Swift Elk and Malpractice McCorckel joined them. Ray looked down at the body of the NVA commander. "If I followed my people's customs I would scalp and mutilate him so he would be a cripple in the afterworld."

Malpractice pointed down at the scabbard on Swift Elk's boot. "There's your knife. Go to work."

But Swift Elk shook his head. "No. I have to admit I respect this man. I think he deserves better than an eternity as a paraplegic. He fought a good battle."

"He was one of the toughest bastards we ever went up against," Falconi said. "The thing that finally did him in was the babbling of a prisoner of war under the influence of sodium pentothal."

"Disjointed babbling, sir," Swift Elk reminded him. "All about bamboo and caves. And from a man actually sent over to our side to fool us."

Falconi pointed over where Archie Dobbs was chatting with Blue Richards. "We might add something about a damned good man in the enemy's rear stumbling across bamboo and caves, too. That made it possible to put it all together."

"Begging your pardon, sir," Top said. "I reckon our stints as commando leaders is over."

"That's right," Falconi said. "You're the top kick of the Black Eagles again."

"Then I'll round 'em up and move 'em out, sir," Top said. "We're wasting time just hanging around here." He turned and bellowed, "All right, you bastards! You've had a ten-minute break. Now fall in! And I mean right now, goddamn it!"

Archie grinned and winked at Blue. "I think the operation is over."

Epilogue

Brigadier General James Taggart took a healthy swig of his coffee, draining the cup. Shoving it aside, he reached across his desk and pulled a cigar from a humidor. After lighting it, he sat back and put his feet up on his desk for a few minutes of relaxation.

He was a craggy-faced officer with features that seemed to have been chiseled out of stone. But now the usual scowl was not there and the general almost displayed a smile. This was one of his favorite times of day. His morning staff meeting had just ended. All the bickering with staff officers—not to mention chewing their asses bloody, plus listening to report after droning report of administration, intelligence, operations, logistics, morale problems, and countless other problems—left him worn out and testy.

These were the fleeting but pleasant few moments every day in which he enjoyed his coffee and cigar, giving him a chance to unwind until the next meeting just after lunch.

His intercom buzzed.

"Shit!" Taggart said. He flipped the button on the instrument. "What is it, Blanchard? And it better be goddamned important!"

"Well, sir," came the voice of his staff duty non-commissioned officer, Master Sergeant Leroy Blanchard.

"There's an officer here from SOG operations—a Major Gray."

Taggart scowled. Now he was getting angry. Just what the hell was a lowly major doing bothering a brigadier general? "What does he want?"

"Uh, sir, the major says he's got a report in from I Corps operations," Blanchard said.

"Now ain't that wonderful?" Taggart remarked. "Tell him I already had my staff meeting."

"Yes, sir," Blanchard said. "But the major says he just now got this here report."

"Then, goddamn it, tell him there's another staff meeting at 1300 hours. I'd love to see his report then."

"Well, sir, the major says he has orders to show it to you now, sir," Blanchard said hesitantly.

"Oh yeah? And who says he's to show it to me *now?*"

"He tells me that the commanding general of U.S. Army Forces Strike Command says so, sir."

"Send him in, Blanchard! Send him in!"

The door opened and Major Gray presented himself with a flourishing salute. "General, I have been dispatched to advise you of a situation that has rapidly developed in the Central Highlands. It's considered an emergency at this point but could be properly rectified if prompt but extremely hazardous action is taken. I also carry orders with me that put you in command of dealing with the situation."

"What situation?" Taggart asked.

"Remote areas of the Central Highlands are being subjected to concentrated and strong hit-and-run attacks by NVA-directed Viet Cong units," the major said. "Their targets have been villages, supply depots, motor pools, roads, and other such objectives."

"That is nothing new, Major!" Taggart growled. He slapped some documents on his desk. "These folders are filled with such situations!"

"The amount and strength of these operations make this quite unique, sir," Major Gray said. "In fact, at first

nothing unusual was noticed. Battalion-sized units were sent in to deal with the situation. But the Viet Cong simply melted away until these large outfits left. Then the enemy renews their efforts."

"I understand now," Taggart said. "So we need a special type of unit to remedy the situation, right?"

"Yes, sir," Gray said.

"From the way you describe things, they would have to be a rather small detachment to go out there and stay out there until the Viet Cong—or themselves—is wiped out, right?"

"I'm afraid so, General," Gray said. "I hate to say so, but actually what is called for is an outfit made up of near-suicidal crazies who would will fight anyone, anywhere, and anyhow." He sighed and shrugged. "Do you know of any group close to that."

Taggart grinned. "Major, I know of an outfit *exactly* like that!"